A TALE OF TWO SISTERS

A WITCH & WIZARD ANTIQUES & MONSTER-HUNTING UNIQUE PARANORMAL MYSTERY NOVELLA - BOOK 1

BETTINA M JOHNSON

AQUA RAVEN PUBLISHING

A Tale of Two Sisters

ISBN: 978-1-7350692-8-9 (paperback)

Cover art by Tina Adams

PROLOGUE

August 1950

The young woman remained listless, curled up on the cot in her cell. Unshed tears burned her eyes as she stared at the stark walls. She'd been in solitary for a week now and knew the nurses were observing her lest she tried to harm herself. They watched her twenty-four hours a day via the tiny windows that lined the opposite wall. She didn't care about that. She didn't care about much these days.

If she closed her eyes, she could see his face. So, she hardly ever closed her eyes, waiting instead for the heavy sedation drugs to take hold and drag her into oblivion. It was a state she preferred over the reality that made her world dark when she was awake. Both of her wrists were bandaged efficiently yet showed the scarring on the edges where she'd cut herself. They placed the cuffs just above the wounds, securing her to either bed rail to prevent her from trying anything else.

She wasn't sure what they expected her to try in a padded cell with a cot, a toilet, and a small sink as her only companions. She didn't even have a pillow or bedding. They came in three times a day and once in the middle of the night to give her medication, food, and allow her a few moments to use the facilities while they stood nearby. There was no such luxury as privacy in the mental hospital.

Her family never came to visit.

Nor did she expect them to—not after what she did to blemish their good name.

No family member ever acted out or did something as lowbrow as to attempt suicide. Better had she succeeded in that attempt. They could have hidden her demise behind some rare and undisclosed disorder which would have expunged any hint of her killing herself from the record books. Her father was that powerful. Her mother even more so, although something had happened to that power since they came here to this country. She didn't know what caused this, however. It was her mother her thoughts drifted to now.

"Better you forget dat boy. Nothing good would have come from dat marriage. Disremember him." Her mother's Caribbean accent always came out when she was distressed or angered. But despite her mother's advice, she knew nothing would ever make her forget Ronald Stewart, her Ronnie. The war took her betrothed away in mere weeks of its onset, leaving her fractured and broken.

No one could soothe her nerves and remove the dagger from her heart. She spent hours crying, wishing she was back in *Sent Lisi*—St. Lucia, wrapped in her grandmother's arms. *Gwanmanman*, the French Patois for grandmother, her favorite person in the entire world, was purported to be a *vyé lam*, a witch, and she often spent weeks with her. At the same time, her mother ran wild with American men who came to her island. Her grandmother would know how to help her.

Her half sisters thought she was an adopted child—the product of some joining between her mother and an

2

unknown man—one their father had adopted despite not being his offspring. She tried to correct them the first time she heard them taunt her about it. "*Mwen sé pa on bata, mwen sé léjitim li.* I'm not a bastard; I'm his legitimate child." But they didn't understand her. They scolded her often and told her to forget the island speak and her heritage and be more like them.

They even teased her about her skin color even though it was similar to theirs. They called her "the little colored girl' until their father caught them at it and scolded them severely. She remembered her grandmother telling her about her family, "*Manman mwen sété chabin èk papa mwen sété bétjé, èk sé pou sa mwen blan kon sa.* My mother was light-skinned and my father was white, and that is why I am so white." But none of this mattered to her now—it never really mattered.

What mattered were the lessons she could learn in the spellbook her grandmother gifted her on her sixteenth birthday, unbeknownst to her parents or sisters. Spells from her heritage, from the islands, and the native people and West Africans brought there, spoke to her. Her people—all of them. She knew she had to bide her time and play the game these doctors expected. Only then would she get her freedom so she could sneak off and study that book, learning everything she could from its pages.

Dark, alluring magic was waiting for her—calling to her. If she could fool the doctors, bide her time, and play the game, she knew she would be free once more. Then she could seek out the answers she needed. Then she could learn the magic of her people.

Keening softly to herself, she hardened her heart.

She would learn all the magic from the book that she could.

Only then could she bring her Ronnie back.

Only then would she indeed be free—especially free from the two sisters.

No prison cell could be worse than being tied to those two.

The two sisters.

CHAPTER 1

"Why did we have to open so early today? We usually open at nine! Whose idea was it to offer an early bird hour before that, for dealers only?" I grumbled to myself, rolling out of bed and hitting the tiny bathroom in my Class C recreational vehicle. My cat, Bob, a tuxedo feline of the extra rotund variety, chirped his sympathies. I noticed he didn't move from his spot on the pillow next to mine.

I rushed through my morning ablutions, grabbing the last piece of breakfast quiche in my equally tiny refrigerator, wolfing it down with a cup of tepid coffee—I definitely needed a new coffee machine. Then added more kibble to Bob's dish.

Some people enjoy the stability of living your life in the town where you were born. From birth onward, you live, work, play, learn, worship, raise a family, grow old and die in a community where you know your friends and neighbors. And family is close by, if not within walking distance.

I am *not* one of those people.

Don't get me wrong. When the holidays roll around, or

I'm in the mood for my Aunt Morwena's famous chili, I'm OK with it. Or if I want to meet with cousins to catch up on family news, going back home to Mystic Valley, North Carolina, is just what I need.

For about two weeks.

Then I'm ready to hit the road, living the nomadic life.

I'm a loner and used to fight with my sister constantly because she was always my shadow. When I would have instead played a solitary game or read a book, she wanted to drag me outside to play with others. We are twins. Not identical, although people insisted we were because, quite frankly, we looked exactly alike. However, I am a flaming redhead, and Ellie was raven-haired.

My name is Maggie Isla Fortune. And Ellie? Ellie Skye Fortune. I was born first, a full ten minutes into the world before they managed to get Ellie out, and I never let her forget it. She forever played the little sister card and got most of the attention. I was OK with that because, yeah, I am *not* needy. She used to complain loudly any time I'd say that. Insisting she wasn't deprived of attention—just enthusiastic and outgoing, while I was a boring old fuddy-duddy.

I'm not quite sure where she picked up that oldie but goodie, but I can assure you, I am very *much* a fuddy-duddy.

Ellie was the life of the party, of that there was no doubt. She had so many friends, I used to run next door to Aunt Morwena's house to escape the noise they would create. But they usually found me and dragged me into their games with Ellie leading the charge. I'd protest, but in actuality, as long as she was in that crowd, I'd be fine.

Ellie told me once that if she only had me for company she'd go insane. I don't think insanity has set in yet, but talk about irony! If we flipped the situation, I'd be better suited to what our life is like now. Why?

Well, unfortunately, Ellie is dead.

I know. Whenever I think about it, I feel sad and guilty and wish I could fix everything back to the way it used to be. Trust me, Ellie agrees *daily*.

Oh! I'm not assuming this, as if she's letting me know somehow from the great beyond. Ellie tells me in person, er, spirit, every day.

You see, Ellie is a ghost.

I am not too astounded by this because my entire family comes from an ancient line of powerful witches and mystics. Our reality *is* paranormal. Although no one in my family believed me when I first told them Ellie was still among the living—just in a floating transparent kind of way.

Yes, witches believe in ghosts, but few of us can see them —it's a rare talent. I can sense them in objects or places, but until Ellie died, I never saw them. Now? All the time. My family doesn't want to hear this because only dark witches have that particular talent, and we don't have many in my family. And last I heard, nope, I'm not a dark witch. And while we don't shun them, my family tends to mistrust them. So, I'm not sure *why* this has happened. Maybe it's a twin thing.

I only know of one close to my age, my cousin, Lily Sweet. When we visited a few weeks back, Lily could not only see Ellie but could speak with her. You can imagine how stunned we were to realize someone else could interact with Ellie in her spooky state. I don't shun dark witches. I think they are fantastic!

"Bob! Leave that alone! It's my last coffee filter."

Bob, unhappy with his diet dry kibble, decided to play head games with me. He didn't think I could see him pawing at the filter. Last week, he did the exact same thing and managed to swipe not only a filter but my Jeep keys into his water dish. He wants real food. Sighing, I tossed him the last of my quiche. Bob always wins.

"You're lucky I'm not a dark witch. I'd turn you into a goldfish."

Cousin Lily has been estranged from the family for a long time and only recently returned. She didn't even know she was a witch growing up! Can you imagine that? I can't conceive how it must have felt discovering to have magical ability so late. I was practically born doing magic, which is rare for our kind. Usually, most young witchlings come into their magical powers around puberty. Not me! My psychic talent manifested when I was three, and it freaked my mother out something awful. Can you imagine how difficult it was trying to raise a child who knew what you were thinking?

All the time?

My power intensifies if I touch something or someone.

Ellie can read auras and make suggestions—mind-bending if you will. She had a promising career going as an antique appraiser and used her talent to keep disgruntled customers from causing trouble. You have no idea how many people think their ten-dollar teacup is worth thousands. Ellie would have been running the family business with my dad by now had she not gotten murdered. Yes, murdered. Some evil monster killed my sister and his capture hasn't occurred yet. Another irony considering what I do for a living.

You see, I belong to a traveling group of paranormal monster-hunters posing as antique appraisers of the outré and unusual. Seriously. Even though we operate in a human world, any bizarre, mystical, or magical item that needs to be appraised, traded, auctioned, exorcised of evil, or destroyed if it's a lost cause, winds up in our caravan of misfits. The Antiques and Mystic Uniques Caravan is my baby. Being part of this highly-classified group comes with many perks, especially when we keep up our quota. And trust me, we get the job done.

Last week, I found two ghosts living in the bottom of a dining room credenza and an imp inside a Barbie doll—something that happens more often than most people realize! Another time, a plethora of fairy-folk took over a lamp—they would light it up and shut it off at will, even with a burned-out lightbulb! I also dealt with a genie, of all things. No. He wasn't in a lamp—he turned himself into a rocking chair and resided in a nursing home. He kept getting frisky any time a sweet old lady would sit down on him—he has a thing for younger women. What? He was over two thousand years old! We finally convinced him to move on or the Biodag would have come for him. They keep our paranormal world running smoothly among all the different Breed—supernatural beings.

The paranormal world has a central organization called The Order of Origin which makes all the laws and keeps the many different Breed, the term used to differentiate us from humans, from running amok. Based in Scotland, it is who the Biodag have to answer to. They are kind of like magical police officers. My group is part of the organization but a separate entity.

We hide in the open operating within my family's business of antiques. The Fortunes are world-renowned antique dealers and travel the globe buying, selling, and appraising the most priceless items. My group tags along with the leading auction house as a dealer of oddities, as I mentioned. When humans come to our tent, we appraise their hundred-year-old puppet or tarot card deck purported to be from the first Romanian gypsy troupe or what have you. But paranormals would seek us out for the magical and mystical artifacts —or to remove an entity from a desired object.

No one wants to bring a demon home hidden in an old truck or vase. Trust me, getting them out of your house can be a real pill.

Occasionally we made mistakes; hey, we were only human!.

Oh, wait.

OK, so even those in the Breed can mess up. I still cringe when I recall the time we inadvertently let an entire army of demented pixies out of their prison and into the world. No, they aren't imaginary beings ascribed to books. Let's just say it took us weeks to round them all up again, and we averted war.

Yes, war.

They tend to go for shiny buttons, and who knew there really was one at the president's disposal. Ok, it's not an actual button, but the pixies moved the hierarchy of command forward with a bit of their mischief. Thankfully, we nabbed the last one before all hell broke loose.

Yeah. I live in a world of freaks and I love it.

However, our primary purpose was to seek out the evil in every town we visited and dispose of them before they could wreak havoc on society. Or continue to, anyway. Loosely regarded as the CIA of the magical world, we operated in stealth since no one knew who we were. Supernatural beings were aware we existed, but I suspect they thought we showed up looking like the cast of Men in Black. They would hardly expect the oddball, ragtag group of merry mischief-makers to be monster-hunters. We appraised antiques for heaven's sake!

And since our job was so dangerous, I kept my family at arm's reach. Dad knew that we were something more than just dealers, but he chose not to ask too many questions knowing his sister had it under control.

Aunt Morwena knows because she was the past leader—I took over when she retired. She recruited me the same year Ellie went into trade with my dad. Ellie, the outgoing one, preferred to be at the home base to stay close to family and friends and was the head of operations there. Had I not been in training, off on one of my distant travels, I might have been here when someone attacked Ellie. Aunt Morwena ordered me not to think such thoughts, but I still feel like I let Ellie down despite her arguing to the contrary.

Guilt made me a better undercover evil-hunting operative. Trust me. Someday I'd use what I've learned on the job to track down and nab the one who made her a ghost. We are a team of ten, with Ellie as our eleventh honorary member—it's not like she has anything else to do.

I'm just glad my crew can see her. We are not sure why this is, but it makes things easy in my world not to have to explain why I speak to the air next to me and nod when it replies. I'm the only one who can *hear* her though. Ellie uses the talents she was born with as a witch, and it comes in handy when we need someone invisible to do reconnaissance for us. We hope to have her back in her corporeal form someday and would figure out what to do about losing our stealth weapon if and when that time comes.

"There you are! I thought I smelled coffee."

Ellie came floating into the RV and hovered by the kitchen sink.

"You fed Bob something naughty again. I can tell. He has a look of supreme smugness on his furry face," Ellie scolded.

"I can't help it! I swear he's part beagle with those sad eyes of his! I'm a bad cat mommy."

"You're not a bad mommy. You're just a sucker. Bob has you wrapped around his tiny cat paw," Ellie laughed.

"Yeah, well, that's the only thing tiny about him!"

Bob was not amused and wandered into the kitchenette to hunt for crumbs then jumped up on the counter where he curled up in the sink, ready for a nap.

"I'm sorry. I polished off the quiche and needed more coffee. It's going to be a long day and..."

"Sis," Ellie stopped my rambling, "please stop. You know I can't eat anything. Now I'm going to head over to our tent and wait for you there. But you need to stop letting that guilty look cross your face every time I mention food. Surely I'm not so petty as to complain when you eat or drink around me. It's all good."

No. It was *not* all good. Ellie deserved her life back and I wanted to be the one to give it to her. Why do I think I can bring her back? Because I'm a Fortune. And we always get what we want. Well, that, and the fact that Ellie isn't technically one hundred percent dead. Instead, she's housed back at the family compound.

Let me explain.

My family of Fortunes, Muirs, and Lupus is vast. Two sisters, Margaret and Moira Muir were both born in Scotland. Margaret married Reginald Croy, and Moira married Robert Fortune. Regie and Moira were our grandparents. The Croys had Iona, Jessica, and Adelaide and they are our Georgia cousins, along with Lily. The Fortunes had Morwena, our aunt, and William, our dad.

Dad is a man of the world. Well-traveled due to a bad case of wanderlust—hence our caravan of sorts—he grew the family business into an empire. Dad met and married our mother, Tassa Lupu, and had us. My mother was Romanian but born in Scotland. Her mother was half Romanian and half Scot. Both of her parents would go back and forth across Europe. They are Romani people—gypsies. Although some consider that title vulgar, we don't and use the word often to describe our clan.

Mom embraced her Scot roots and gave us Gaelic names: Eilidh—Ellie, and Magaidh, or Maggie.

With our parents joining cultures, it was almost natural that we took up the gypsy lifestyle. Ellie and I are American. Our parents settled in North Carolina for a time and had us, then started getting that itch again. Our business became more mobile, and my dad got to travel the world once more. Our mom got to get away from her people, which caused trouble when she moved to North Carolina. We don't know much about our Romanian side, except both of mom's parents died young. And she ran off with my dad partially because she fell in love with him, but also to escape her Lupu family—apparently, not a nice bunch. Mom never spoke about them.

We lost our mom five years ago to cancer.

Most of the Fortune side of the family has psychic ability and are witches. I have photoscopic tendencies, as did Ellie. We can touch items and know much about them by holding them, like provenance and past ownership. We also have retrocognitive abilities—I can hold onto an object and be thrust back in time, seeing the people and places involved with the piece I am holding. I tend to walk around wearing gloves so I could remain here in the present. You can imagine how sought out I am in our paranormal antique world. My witchy abilities are strong, and I can hold my own, though I rarely like to use magic.

One day this item showed up. We don't know who brought it, but he left a note with instructions for us to find the piece's provenance and left a large chunk of gold as payment. We suspected he was Romanian because they usually deal in gold or jewels and not cash. It was a small statue of a crouching wolf.

The minute Ellie touched it she knew very dark magic was at play. She saw a man holding the statue in one hand and using a sword to stab another through the heart, effectively murdering him—then running off with the piece. She could only describe the man who died because it was as if she was seeing through the eyes of the murderer. When the man came to pick up the little wolf statue, he remained in shadows, disguising himself and making my father suspicious. My dad, convinced he was with the murderer, threatened to call the Biodag, so the man ran off, never to be seen again.

We thought everything would be fine, but one day Ellie was alone at our home base in Mystic Valley, and the man returned. He found Ellie by herself and grabbed her, demanding the return of the statue. We are unsure of what Breed we were dealing with, but he drained Ellie of her powers. When she refused to help and threatened to scream, he slammed horribly vile dark magic into her. When we came back from our outing, we found her dead, and the statue gone.

Well, I say dead because Ellie had no pulse, no beating heart, and was for all intents and purposes dead. But her body would not decompose! It remained as if in a trancelike state—like a coma. She looked like a lifeless, beautiful doll. My family didn't know what to make of this. They feared burying her in case this was some kind of weird magic that could be reversed. So they encased Ellie in a glass coffin, like Snow White, where she remains to this day. Safely tucked at our home base with guardians watching over her. Indeed, my Aunt Morwena barely ever leaves her home and guards the basement door like Cerberus guarding the entrance to the underworld.

About four weeks after Ellie 'passed,' she showed up in ghost form and nearly scared me out of my skin. There you have it. With most of my family refusing to believe my ability to see and hear Ellie, we just got back to our way of life.

However, we're on a mission, my entire crew that is, to find the man that did this and bring him to justice. Maybe it will release the hold he has on Ellie's spirit so she can move on to her next life, or perhaps come *back* to life again. We scour the earth hoping to find someone wise in our world who may know what kind of dark magic consumes her.

Lily promised to ask her great-grandmother, Adriana—on her father's side of the family, to see if she had possible answers. But they are dealing with their *own* family drama, which leaves little time for ours. Hopefully, Lily will clear up her mess so she can help us.

We shall see.

Right now, I was hoping for one more cup of joe before starting my day. With Ellie whisking away, leaving me to my thoughts, I knew I had to get a move on, or I'd be late. I filled my carafe and went to grab a muffin that I'd hidden in the cabinet knowing I'd shove it in my face the second Ellie was gone. It wasn't meant to be, however, as the door of my RV crashed open, startling me out of my reverie.

Bob just opened one eye then rolled over.

"Are you going to spend the morning daydreaming? Or will you help us set up the tents? We open soon, you know."

Ah! Nathara. Lovely. Unlike my cousin, Lily. Nathara was a dark witch that I did not find fascinating. As a matter of fact, I disliked her so much I would prefer to punch her in the nose. Daily. The last thing I needed was for her to mess with me first thing in the morning.

"I was communing with nature and centering myself, as you well know. I need to do this before handling so many items, or I will go mad."

"All I see is someone staring into a cup of coffee. But if that's what you call centering. Plus, you are already mental, so what other excuse will you use?"

Grr. Did I mention I dislike Nathara?

CHAPTER 2

"What's up her butt?" I had my table set up and was rushing around getting the last bit of detail arranged that made for a good reading so I could welcome my first client.

There was a reasonably long line of customers patiently waiting on me—some human. Still, I thought I detected a few paranormal mixed in. There was at least one vampire in line. They usually stood out because they wore very dark sunglasses and large hats. Vampires, the old ones anyway, could handle being in the sunlight, but they avoided it whenever possible.

"I don't know, Maggie. Nathara has been prickly ever since we came back from Miami. I think she met a man down there, had a fling, but now regrets it. Or she expected a bit more from the guy, but he hasn't called her since. That has to rub her wrong," Ellie commented.

My sister spent most of her time flitting back and forth from tent to tent, keeping tabs on the goings-on, then reporting to me in case someone in my crew needed me in a hurry. Otherwise, she hangs out in the tent I share with Bella.

I stay on one side where I handle and appraise all manner of genuinely bizarre items. Bella gets those looking for a bit of fun with their appraisal, so she offers a cup of tea and a free tarot reading as a bonus for humans and paranormals.

Ours was a popular tent.

Bella is the comic relief of our group, although we don't think that is her real name. She is an elemental. I am not sure precisely what this means, and she doesn't offer up any explanation that we can comprehend. Still, she is probably the deadliest hunter in our team, not that anyone would believe it. She looks and acts like a petulant teenager with an attitude to spare. Usually wearing her golden-brown hair in pigtails, few would think she is ancient, mistakenly believing her to be sixteen if that. Her skin is a warm golden-brown in a forever tan. Her eyes are a unique amber color I don't think any average human would ever sport. She literally has the same color hair, skin, and eyes. She reminds me of those California girls and is a charming imp.

"Well, Nathara needs to stay clear of me for the rest of the day because I woke up grumpy, and I'm looking for someone to tussle with," I groused.

"You just want an excuse to slug her. Everyone knows it. We've taken bets to see how long you last," Bella chuckled. "Just give me a heads up, and I'll hold her for you."

Bella wasn't a fan of our dark witch either.

With my disposition, I expect those that bet sooner rather than later would see some cash in their pockets shortly. My red-headed bad temper is legendary among the group.

"You ready?" Bella stood to pull the cord that would open the front flap and signal that we were open for business.

"Yep! Go ahead and pull it."

"I AM THINKING LATE fourteenth century or early fifteenth. It must be priceless, no?"

The woman sitting in front of me had such an earnest look on her face, I had difficulty coming up with the words I knew would shatter any visions of wealth that she had. She brought in a sword which she said had been in her family for quite some time. Her father told all three siblings that their grandfather acquired it on one of his journeys worldwide. It was a sword used in magic acts for sword swallowing, a flamberge serpentine sword, one hundred percent real. However, this sword was made in the 1950s and was only worth about two hundred dollars. Had it been a fourteenth-century sword, the price tag would be upwards of thirty thousand dollars.

I made eye contact with Ellie, and she positioned herself behind the woman, ready to make a 'suggestion' should things get out of hand.

"Well, I am sure this is a treasure for your family, and it is a beautiful sword. It looks like, if you notice the tiny marking here on the side, that it was manufactured right here in the United States and, my goodness! I believe you have a genuine movie prop, circa nineteen fifty or so! Definitely a neat family heirloom and would probably fetch around three hundred or so at auction."

"But my daddy... he said this was a priceless treasure from the Far East or some other Godforsaken place! Maybe I need someone more seasoned and experienced to have a look at this piece. You obviously don't understand what I have here!" I watched her eyes as Ellie went to work and looked on in wonder as my irate client suddenly became calm and pleasant once more.

"Oh! And a movie prop. Won't my kids love that! Both my boys are movie buffs and love all those old forties and fifties swashbuckling flicks. Hey! Maybe they used this sword in one of them!"

And just like that, I was out of deep doo-doo and sent my satisfied customer on her merry way.

"Thanks, sis."

"Don't mention it, Mags." Ellie smiled, shaking her head at how simple it was for her to influence an outcome with the barest of suggestions. That was usually a talent vampires employed. Freaky my sister could do it with ease.

I scarcely had time to reset myself and prepare for my next customer when I felt a sudden chill in the air, so much so that I gasped aloud. Looking up quickly, I drew back when the figure of a rather large man entered the tent and came into the light of my lamp. He was indeed a vampire. Sans the floppy hat and sunglasses, but there was no mistaking a full-blooded vamp, and an ancient one at that.

He nodded at me and glanced over at Bella, who was occupied with her customer and paid us no mind. Taking a seat, he gingerly removed a small item out of his pocket and placed it on the table in front of me.

The power emanating from it was palpable, and I felt the hair rise on the back of my neck.

"What is that?" I asked before I caught myself.

"That's what I was hoping you could tell me," the vampire stated, giving me the barest of smiles.

"May I?" I asked, waiting for his nod in the affirmative before I reached out to grasp the item in my palm. I felt a passing tremor of some manner of ancient magic. I knew I'd need to remove my leather gloves and hold the bowl against my bare flesh to get an accurate idea of what I was dealing with. Again, making eye contact with Ellie, I turned to watch as Bella's customer left the tent, all smiles and clutching a bit of cash in her hand.

"Bella? Can you hold off bringing in your next client? I have something here."

Bella nodded, giving my vampire the once over then wandered over to the tent flap to bar anyone from entering.

We usually had a routine like this. When one of us got a hit on something paranormal, or an apparent Breed came in looking for our services, the other would stop everything, keeping looky-loos from entering our tent. So far, it has worked like a charm.

Slipping my glove from my hand, I placed the item in my palm once more. Instantly, I transported from my tent to an arid landscape where many people were chanting and swaying. I looked down at the item and noticed it was no longer in my hand but on a stone tableau before me, and I held a rudimentary knife possibly made out of a bear tooth. I watch with interest as I held out my hand and used the knife to slice open my palm. I observed the blood drip down into the tiny object that, upon closer inspection, looked to be a bat with wings wrapping around a catch basin or bowl. The bat's tongue was out as if it were preparing to lap my blood as the basin filled.

I looked up at the people to better read who they might be and watched in fascination as a look of horror came over a man closest to me. He appeared to be a shaman, and I believed I was gazing at native people, tribe unknown. I was startled when he shouted at me.

"Átahsaia!"

The music stopped. The people who were singing and swaying did as well. All eyes now on me, each person repeated what the old shaman stated.

"Átahsaia! Átahsaia!"

I closed my eyes and allowed myself to tumble back to the present and sat a moment blinking, more than a bit dizzy as I tried to get my bearings.

I looked around the room and noticed not only had the vampire sat back in shock, but Bella was standing by my side with a look of alarm on her face. Ellie was fluttering around, looking concerned.

"What happened?" I asked.

"You tell me!" Bella replied, glancing at the vampire.

"I kind of got sucked into another time, I guess. I think this is a tribal bowl. I need to look something up if you have a moment more," I told the vampire, who appeared intrigued by my words. He nodded yes, and I proceeded to pull my laptop toward me as I began typing various spellings of the name I'd heard. It took a few tried until I nailed it.

"Bingo! It's Zuni. This item seems to be a collection bowl for a ritual, a blood ritual. I heard the tribe chanting a name, Átahsaia. He is a Zuni cannibalistic demon who was a giant. Often depicted as fully humanlike with long silver hair, he is extremely tall, taller than any man. Some of that hair could be as sharp as a porcupine. He also supposedly had a mouth that stretched grotesquely from ear to ear with yellowed bar-like tusks poking out of it. He sounds charming," I laughed.

The vampire smiled indulgently and asked what I knew regarding the little bat bowl or if it remained an enigma.

"Not much. I mean, I would have to do a bit more research, but several similar items show to be selling between three hundred and eight hundred dollars. However, from what I can tell, this appears to be an effigy bowl. See this example online? It is a Zuni frog effigy bowl. This little bat is similar in appearance, except I've never seen a bowl with wings stretched around it like this except for Cherokee Indian bowls. I am almost wondering if this one has ties to both tribes. I would think the Oklahoma Cherokee may have come into contact by trade with the Zuni people, so maybe this is a hybrid of sorts. In any case, it is unique and holds no negativity that I can sense, despite the blood connection."

"Oh, but that is why I purchased it. I have no intention of selling. I just wanted verification of the blood ritual aspect. I do treasure anything to do with such a topic, you know."

Yeah, being a vampire, I could see why he'd have a blood fetish—pun intended. After a few more uneventful appraisals, I was getting itchy for a break. I was just about to suggest one when in walked two elderly ladies holding a lamp. They introduced themselves as Esther and Louise Birch.

"Like the tree, dear. Only we aren't trees."

Right.

"This is our sister Millicent."

I looked around for a third sister but didn't see another person with them.

"Um, sister?"

"The lamp, dear. Millicent."

Okay then.

"How may I, um, help you?" I had no idea where this was going. I was ninety-nine percent positive I was dealing with two slightly befuddled old ladies. I wasn't getting a paranormal vibe, but you never knew. I heard Bella chuckling to my left and tossed her a stern look.

"We need you to convince Millicent to come out of the lamp and tell us where her body is so we can bury her."

What do you say to that? I must have looked as confused as I felt because one of the sisters, Louise, I believe, began to pat my hand in a 'there, there' kind of way.

"Millicent doesn't want to get buried you see."

No, I did not see.

Why did I always get the loopy ones? I mean, these little old ladies seemed nice enough, but really? A lamp? A possessed one?

"Perhaps I should examine the lamp?" Bella was wiping her eyes and excused herself. I could tell she was struggling to hold in a laugh. Even Ellie followed her out of the tent—the traitor.

I sat forward and gingerly picked up the lamp, expecting to find nothing much more than a few fleeting glimpses of its past.

Boy, was I ever wrong.

I found myself whisked to a grand room in an ancient house. I was standing in the middle of what appeared to be a Victorian-style home and was in between the formal living and dining rooms. Looking around, I could just make out the furniture and décor from the light filtering in the windows. It appeared to be early evening or late afternoon. If I turned to my right and walked diagonally, I would be in the entry foyer, so that is what I did.

Peering into the room on the other side of the foyer, I found myself gazing at wall-to-wall books—a library. There was a large ornate desk in front of a colossal fireplace and a globe bar sitting beside it. On the opposite wall were two picture windows and beneath them was a window seat. Sitting on the window seat was the figure of a woman in a long woolen dress. Her grey hair was up in a severe bun, but her face was in shadow.

"Millicent?" I whispered my inquiry.

The woman didn't move a muscle except to turn her head in my direction, giving me a good look at her, then began to shriek.

I plunged back to reality.

"What the heck was that?" I uttered before I could censor myself.

The two sisters looked at one another knowingly.

"That was Millicent."

CHAPTER 3

I sent the elderly sister duo on their way, the lamp tucked safely in Esther's tote, with promises that I'd have an answer for their little problem in a few hours. They asked that I stop by their home the next day and gave me a spare key even! What else could I do? I needed to call a group meeting because nothing like this had ever happened to me before and we needed to strategize.

I mean, if that screaming specter on the window seat was Millicent, I didn't know how I would help her or her sisters find peace. Not without information. A lot more information.

"Go over everything again. You said you were whisked inside the Birch family home, a Victorian. And as you went from room to room, you came upon a ghost?" Antoine asked me as I sat down under the awning of my RV. We were grilling lunch, and I told my tale to those collected as best I could, all things considered. Sometimes I became disoriented for hours after such a vivid experience, and I was still a bit shaky.

Antoine is a vampire. Enough said. Well, except that he is acting head of our division since none of my team knows I am the true leader. I chose to remain incognito—just another member of the team. I didn't want the group to think I got the job because I'm a Fortune. I had to work incredibly hard to move up to this position, but I knew some would wonder. *And I mean* you *Nathara!* Antoine is extremely tall, as most vampires tend to be. Handsome, with dark brown skin and piercing blue eyes, he forever hides behind sunglasses, even at night. He wears his long hair braided back and favors bolero hats. He rarely smiles, but when he does, he has the world's cutest dimples I've ever seen on a man.

"I CAN'T TELL you how weird that was, knowing I was safe in my tent doing a reading... but when that thing began shrieking like a banshee, all I wanted to do was hightail it out of there and hide under my bed! And I'm not one for dramatics. It's just that, well, she had no face. Where her face should have been was a blank oval. No eyes. No nose. No mouth. Yet she managed to open something to make that shrieking noise. Ugh, I am so wigged out." I explained.

Ellie was rubbing my back as she hovered nearby.

"And it's not like ghosts freak me out," I added, jerking my thumb over my shoulder to point out the obvious. Ellie just smiled as most everyone else chuckled.

"What was it about the situation then, to make you turn into a scaredy-cat?" Nathara asked snidely, adding a little tsk at the end to show how ridiculous she felt my reaction was.

The woman is as slippery and viper-like as the snake; that is the meaning behind her cognomen. But she certainly has a stellar track record of eliminating threats in our world. So I tolerate her attitude, which is usually dialed toward bitchy.

We tended to stay away from each other most days, but this was no ordinary day. Nathara pulled her long inky black hair back and squinted at me. Her pale skin reminds me of moonlight, and she was wrapped in a sweater despite the warm day. She has bewitching lilac eyes and men usually tripped over themselves when she passed by.

Nathara likes it that way.

I chose to ignore her snarky attitude and answered honestly.

"I felt abject fear and a sensation of hopelessness and despair. I felt all my senses kick in, and my flight reflex won over reason. Every fiber of my being reacted, warning me to get the heck out of there. So that's what I did."

"Come here, darling. I'll give you a hug and make the bad feeling go away," Johnny offered with a growl in his voice.

Johnny was eye-candy. There. I said it. He was a seducer of the maleficent and evil witch variety. No one could rack up supernatural cougars on a mission of destruction like our Johnny. He's a werewolf. I know. How sexy is that? He knew his way around an array of weapons but chose not to carry any on a mission, preferring to shift into his wolf form instead. He looked like a lithe version of Wolverine with the blackest eyes I've ever seen on a man. His Italian complexion made many in the female persuasion swoon just by him casually walking by. Shocking white teeth and a knowing smile...no one would suspect that come the full moon, he's quite a different animal. Yet for all that, Johnny has a heart of gold and is the big brother I always wanted—I just wish he'd stop shedding!

I gave him a soft smile but then shuddered at the memory.

"But you were never in any danger because you weren't there in actuality." This from Tor. I found myself tongue-tied in the most annoying way.

"Uh..."

"Oh, great. Not only is she a scaredy-cat. She's an imbecile. Answer the man! What's with the grunt?" Nathara chastised.

I wanted to wring her neck.

Tor is Johnny's partner in crime and the newest member of our troupe. For some reason, he is the one who gave me the most trouble. But not because he did anything obnoxious. He made my heart do weird little flips every time I sensed him coming near, you see, and I refuse to acknowledge this. I have too much responsibility for that kind of distraction. His full name is Torquil MacDonald, and he is a Scot, like me. He happens to be a sorcerer. We also suspect he is half-vampire. However, Antoine hasn't verified this for me yet.

Tor is tall, more on the average side than reaching the extreme heights Antoine favored. He too was lithe and made one think of Highlander, kilts, and haggis—but in a good way. Or a swashbuckler. Or a... *yeah.* He had hazel eyes and reddish-brown hair that he wore longish and tied back. He also seems to have a perpetual five o'clock shadow that I found disturbingly sexy. He worked in tandem with Johnny, but unlike our wolfie, Tor preferred carrying a deadly-looking magical sword.

"No, I, uh...I realize I wasn't in danger. It's just that I felt such a sinister presence and very dark magic and I recoiled instinctually. I feel better now that I'm...um..." I managed to respond finally, though not intelligently.

"What about the sisters? Did they have a back story for you? Any further explanation as to what happened to Millicent?" Dara queried, deftly stepping in and aiding me before I continued looking and sounding like an eejit, unable to remain cool when queried by the rugged Scot. I owed her one.

"They did. Esther and Louise Birch are twin sisters but not identical, like Ellie and me. Their parents married young and had them a year after they celebrated their first anniversary. Mr. Birch was the town pharmacist and they lived a well-off lifestyle enjoying the finer things in life. He became somewhat famous for his special elixirs, purported to heal everything from the common cold to tuberculosis. All was perfect until Mrs. Birch *died* of tuberculosis, leaving the pharmacist a widower with two ten-year-old daughters to raise. It seems not even his elixirs could save the woman."

Dara nodded encouragingly and handed me a lemonade.

Daracha, Dara for short, is our resident druid with a sidekick who lives inside a crystal ball—we are not sure what Madame Myna is all about. But she is very good at predicting things from inside her tiny round, glass home so we tend to humor her. Dara makes quite a bit of money doing her crystal ball schtick for tourists. Only they think Madame Myna is a Disney prop. We don't disabuse them of that notion. Dara is from Wales originally and has rosy cheeks and curly brown hair laced with silver. She has laugh lines and a great sense of humor but tends to be a loner, like me.

"Tis a pity, that," she stated morosely. Then nodded for me to go on.

"Well, about two years later, Mr. Birch took another wife who came with her own daughter, Millicent. Mr. Birch adopted her, but she is not a blood relation to Esther and Louise. This marriage and adoption were strange for the day because the woman he married must have had some Caribbean island blood in her and had darker skin than the sisters. So did the little girl. Esther and Louise had no idea where their father met the woman or when suspecting he must have when he went on one of his yearly travels abroad. Yet he comes home one day announcing this woman was his wife and they had a new sister. Millicent was about four when she moved in with her mother. All three girls grew into teens, then young women. All three never married. But out of the three, Millicent came closest to tying the knot. Her young man died in the first few days of the United States entering the Korean War. He left his hometown and was lost somewhere near North Korea. He was on a supply boat that hit a mine that was blown to bits."

"Millicent became despondent and had to be medicated for the rest of her life due to severe depression. There were some whispers that he hadn't died, but his family found out Millicent had mixed blood and refused to let the union take place so made up the story that he had passed. Her fiancée's mother and sister were incredibly horrible to Millicent and forbade her from entering their home to give her condolences and commiserate in their shared loss. It broke the girl, being treated as such a lowly creature, but no one could say for sure if the family lied about his demise. They soon moved a few towns away and lost contact with the Birch family. Millicent was supposedly never the same after the incident and remained under her older sisters' care.

"Esther and Louise honored their father's wish by taking care of Millicent and giving her a home until she or they, died. And here is the unbelievable part of the story. A few weeks ago, Millicent was alive, and for all intents and purposes, well. She was eighty-four to Esther and Louise's ninety if you can imagine! But she told the twins that she discovered her beloved was alive, and she intended to reconnect with him even if it were too late for them to marry."

I paused here as everyone in my group began to murmur over the story I was telling, and Bella zoomed in on her roller skates, grabbing a hotdog as she flew by.

"I'll be right back! Are you still telling the story? Ok.

Good! I'm closing up shop." And she spun away, looking every bit the teenager she wasn't.

Clearing my throat to get everyone's attention again, I continued. "The next day after this revelation, the two sisters had a doctor's appointment and upon their return to their home, they discovered Millicent had passed away. She was lying on her bed quite dead with no sign of a struggle or anything to make them believe she killed herself. Millicent appeared to be asleep as if she'd taken a nap and never woke up. Before they could call an ambulance to take her body to the hospital for an autopsy, she, well, Millicent, disappeared. You can imagine how the two sisters reacted to this occurrence.

"About a week after that incident, Louise was sitting at the desk in the library. When she turned on the lamp, Millicent made her presence known to them by shrieking. Every time either of the two Birch sisters touches the lamp, they get the same response—loud shrieking by Millicent. I was the only one so far who held the lamp and saw anything, due to my talent as it is."

"And they never found her body?" Sven, another of my team members, asked. "For that matter, did they ever call the authorities or anyone to help them with this situation? Household staff?"

I shook my head no.

"They are aware of the paranormal world even though they, themselves, are not paranormal... that I could suss out anyway," I added.

"It is intriguing," Serena stated softly, looking at her sister. Sydney nodded yes while pulling on her bottom lip before responding. "I wonder if they have a touch of mage or witch in them. Perhaps I can tell when we arrive at their home."

Being Succubi, Serena and Sydney were the most adept at sniffing out those in our world who were trying to conceal the fact they were magical—something that very rarely got past those two, if ever. There's not much you can hide from a minor demon. We occasionally called on Serena and Sydney to enchant and entice the male population of evildoers that needed elimination. Otherwise, they are our principal appraisers. Sexy, tall, model thin, and blonde, with the longest legs no woman should have the right to, they work in tandem with Bella who tends to go for the pervy dudes who like them young. Serena and Sydney are also weapons masters, far surpassing both Johnny and Tor. And they are sharpshooters—hey, sometimes we needed to use guns!

Bella came rushing back on her roller skates and swung into a lawn chair, her mouth stuffed with the remnants of her hotdog.

"Wha nid di miz?" she asked, indelicately, as she munched away.

"Ugh. Didn't your mother ever tell you not to speak with food in your mouth?" Nathara complained.

Bella took a moment to finish chewing loudly, then swallowed before answering. "Perhaps, but she's been gone for well over a thousand years now. I might need a refresher—or not," she sniffed. I noticed she didn't say 'died.' Just 'gone.' I really had to try to get Bella to explain elementals to me.

Turning to Bella, I informed her we were wrapping up the story and needed to decide what our next move should be. "I vote we go to the Birch home since the sisters have invited us. Plus, we have a few days off before we move on to Knoxville."

We left Miami, Florida, and had been winding our way upwards to North Carolina via Georgia, then Alabama, and now we were in Tennessee.

"Who died and made you the boss? I thought that was Antoine's role?" Nathara again.

"Considering her family gives us employment and

graciously lets us spend our off-season living on their land, rent-free, you may want to reconsider your attitude, Nathara," Sven uttered softly.

A Swedish shifter with a military buzz cut to his light blonde hair, Sven is tall and thin, with an almost skeletal build. A shifter is similar, yet different, from a werewolf. Shifters can mimic things. They transform into objects, animals, and even people. Unlike the werewolf, who has a symbiotic relationship with their inner beast, Sven was a master assassin before a near-fatal accident had him incarcerated and up for execution. He chose to accept employment with the Order to get out of jail.

I think he made a wise choice.

Nathara just rolled her eyes and slowly slinked her way across our gathering place, taking a seat near Tor. I narrowed my eyes but kept my mouth shut. Difficult, since my red-haired Scottish hot temper fought to bite back with a nasty retort. Levelheaded coolness won out for now.

Ellie fluttered over to me and asked, "What will happen if I show up at their home with you? Do you think this specter is dangerous? Will it pose a danger to me since I am a ghost?" she asked excitedly. She wrung her hands and looked around at the gathering. She seemed more eager rather than worried, and I suspected she was hoping we'd send her in there to tackle the entity by herself.

That wasn't going to happen.

I informed everyone of Ellie's concerns, and Antoine smiled at my sibling before replying. "I believe we shall scope out this abode first and see what we find... you shall stay in Maggie's vehicle until we give the all clear, my dear. There is no sense in asking for trouble since we have no idea what is going on with this other ghost. If she is in fact, a ghost, and we aren't dealing with something evil."

"What could be worse?" I wondered aloud.

"Banshees. Poltergeists. There are far worse beings out there than a simple haunting spirit," Dara stated ominously. I nodded sagely for Dara was correct, and I knew this.

Well. This will be a fun outing.

Maybe.

CHAPTER 4

I woke early the following day and had already downed a cup of coffee before a knock on my door alerted me to the fact it was time to head out. A few of my crew would ride with me in my old Jeep Grand Wagoneer that I kept hitched to the back of my RV. The rest would ride with Sven.

I fed Bob, brewed another pot of coffee, and prepared for our day.

Antoine didn't have to alert anyone from the main antique troupe of our extracurricular activities. The others in my team failed to comprehend that Antoine answered to me—and I already informed the legit end of operations of our intent.

My family had gravitas. The Fortunes, along with the Muirs and even the Croys, had positions of power the world over. My father, well aware of my career, spent most of his time acquiring new rare antiques and left the mundane to the second in command, Estelle and her husband, Dale. They heard from me and our plans late last night. We would investigate this morning and open for business after lunch.

What no one, not even Antoine realized, was just how high up in the organization I was. My boss was technically in Scotland, and he had recently given me the United States. Like, I am the top-level operative, and there is no one higher. Yeah, it's good to be king, er, queen, rather.

It wasn't all sunshine and roses, however. I'm convinced the weight of responsibility was aging me daily. The lives of my team and those we protected were a constant encumbrance.

"Good morning, sis. Ready to play Ghostbuster?" Ellie was happily drifting, her excitement at our little side project evident. She lived for our true purpose, um, if Ellie were still among the living, that is.

I held up my super-sized travel mug in response.

"That much coffee is going to make you jittery."

"No, this much coffee is going to keep me from killing Nathara if... no, when she gets on my last nerve," I replied.

"Just make her sit way in the back," Ellie laughed.

That's not how we settled in my old Jeep. I drove—hey, it's my vehicle after all—with Antoine in front, Bella between us. Dara was in the back on the bench seat with Sydney and Serena. Our gear was in the cargo area. The two succubae never complained about having to ride with us although I suspect they preferred their own company and would have rather popped in and out of existence and shown up at the old Victorian in their own way.

Johnny, Tor, and Nathara followed in Sven's Jeep Wrangler. What can I say? We liked Jeeps. Ellie would hang with them in her ghost form and keep tabs on Nathara.

Climbing in my vehicle, I noticed Dara had brought Madame Myna along, who was swirling around her crystal ball prison, her face peering out then dissipating into tendrils of smoke before she'd reappear looking in a different direction. She seemed agitated and restless.

"What's wrong with Madame?" I asked.

Dara rolled her eyes, sighing her response. "Madame thinks we are heading for certain danger. Like what else is new? I tried, yet again, to explain that it was our job to head into dangerous situations to fight evil. Still, she always goes on about vigilante justice and letting someone else handle monster-fighting duties so that we can remain safe."

Dara gave the crystal ball a stern look but followed up with a fond pat on its shiny top. "Madame wants to retire to Florida and spend all day on a boardwalk handing out sage advice to tourists. I told her I wasn't even remotely ready to throw in the towel and settle down with something so tame."

Dara had her curly brown hair pulled back into her usual ponytail. Bella did the same to hers, and Antoine had his trademark black low crown bolero hat on, covering his braided hair. His sunglasses shaded his eyes. It might be more comfortable sitting in the front so his long legs could stretch out, but the chatter that would soon ensue from Bella already had him on edge.

She knew her constant prattle irritated the ancient vamp, and I suspected that was why she gave us an endless stream of it. Plus, she tended to lean on Antoine or even rest her head on his shoulder while she let her lips flap. The look he gave me when he found out she was riding with us was priceless. Maybe he'd finally blow his top and show some emotion—I chuckled at the thought and doubted even Bella could ruffle his feathers.

Nathara gave me a smug smile when she passed by, and I knew it had to do with the fact that she was riding with Sven, Johnny, and Tor. I hadn't done anything to make the others suspect my insides fluttered every time Tor came near me, but I wouldn't put it past that woman to figure it out in some weird witchy way. I shook my head and decided not to dwell on it.

Nathara was being Nathara.

Tor nodded as he passed, and I gave him a lame smile and waved back. Ugh. The butterflies started, so I barked at everyone to hurry up.

Antoine turned slightly, addressing the gang. "Ok, here is how we will handle this. I want Maggie, Bella, and me to go in first. Everyone else will hang back and stay on the outside of the house while surrounding it. We need a witness to anything that might be trickery—smoke and mirrors. But I suspect after what Maggie experienced, we are dealing with the paranormal. I've already briefed the others and wanted to update you as well. We don't know what we are walking into, so let's stay alert."

Our drive to the next town was uneventful, and I stayed mindful of the speed limit as I drove through, looking for the landmarks the two Birch sisters gave me in their directions. As I turned left on Hemlock Lane, an eerie sense of déjà vu came over me which only intensified as I pulled into the driveway of number forty-two.

Peering through the windshield, I examined the large Victorian which looked like it had been well-maintained over the years but still gave off a sense of neglect—or maybe it was loneliness. It just seemed to cry out that it was empty except for the ghosts of the past. Or maybe my imagination was running amok, especially since everyone else commented on how lovely it was.

I heard Sven pulling in behind us and rushed out to head Ellie off if she felt the need to disobey our orders to stay put until we understood better what we were dealing with since I had no idea. In my haste, I smacked right into Tor, who'd gotten out and in my way, before I'd realized it.

"Oof. Oh! I'm sorry. I didn't see you there." Obviously. Sheesh, could I get more awkward around this man?

"No worries, lass." Tor smiled down at me and looked to

continue to comment when Nathara managed to slither between us, casting me a derisive glance as she chastised me.

"How do you accomplish it? You always manage to stumble your way into embarrassing situations with seemingly endless abandon. I think it's your superpower." Snickering, Nathara glanced coquettishly at Tor then danced away and over to Antoine.

"I was just checking on Ellie and, um, didn't see you'd already moved out and over to me."

"Maggie, lass, it's fine. It's not often I get run down by such a lovely visage," Tor replied.

Oh, jeez. He's smooth. I gulped, smiled thinly, and hurried around him to head off Ellie who had floated out of the Jeep and was scrutinizing the house with interest.

"You need to wait here...or better yet, go sit in my Wagoneer and wait for us to signal it's fine for you to enter the house. Please, Ellie? I don't know what we are going to find in there."

Giving me a dark look, Ellie grumbled as she floated past me and slipped through the door of my vehicle where she seemed to settle behind the wheel, arms crossed with an annoyed look on her face. She didn't like being left out of all the fun as she called it.

"Ok, everyone. Let's spread out, Antoine instructed. Set up your equipment on the porch and start getting readings. Maggie, Bella, and I will go in first. The sisters said they'd be away this morning but would be back before noon so we have the place to ourselves. Nathara, take Sven and scout the backyard, making sure no one comes in or leaves. We need to rule out any hijinks before we decide if this is a paranormal situation or it becomes apparent that there is no other explanation."

Oh, it was going to be paranormal. I could already sense

an evil presence. Just another day of taking care of bad things in our world it seems.

What fun.

CHAPTER 5

"*W*hat in the holy heck do we have here?" Bella asked.

Indeed. The minute I crossed the threshold and into the home, a soft keening began filtering through the rooms, circling us with a sense of impending doom. The hairs on my body stood at alert, and I shivered. Even as I allowed myself to feel the emotions of fear, I became super focused and excited about the hunt for evil. It's what I was born to do, and my anticipation of solving this bit of intrigue wouldn't allow my nerves to falter.

I was in control.

"It's definitely the home I visited in my vision," I told the others. "I saw the faceless woman in this room to our left. She was sitting on the window seat, but I don't see anything there now." My quick perusal of the front foyer and rooms on the other side belied my words, for nothing seemed to be lurking except for a few buzzing flies who lazily circumvented the room to our left in search of an escape route back outside. The keening lessened ever so slightly, and it certainly wasn't coming from a banshee. I'd heard that sound more times than I cared to count. This was different.

Walking into the library, the first thing I did was open the window seat. I don't know what I expected to find, but it was wide open now—and empty.

"Were you expecting a body?" Bella laughed.

"You know I love *Arsenic and Old Lace*. Cary Grant was his comedic best in that movie. And heck, a body could very well be laid out in this thing—it's huge," I replied. Bella and I had watched the classic movie this past October when it aired around Halloween. It was one of my favorites.

Antoine walked over to an ornately carved wooden desk and glanced at the lamp on it. "Is this the one that is supposed to be possessed by Millicent?" he asked.

"Yes. That's the one the sisters brought yesterday. Why?"

"No reason." Antoine reached out, plugged it into the wall socket, and then pulled the brass chain dangling under the shade. It turned on, rather unremarkable, and didn't seem like an item that held any evil spirit. The keening was barely noticeable now.

"I'm not picking up on anything in this room," Bella stated.

We left the library and crossed the foyer. We were about to enter the opposite room when we heard a commotion behind us on the front porch and Dara rushed in, clutching her oversized handbag to her chest with Madame Myna swirling around in her crystal ball, safely tucked inside.

"Dara! I said to wait outside until we understood our situation," Antoine scolded.

"Well, we have a situation, and you'd better come outside."

"No need for that, folks. Perhaps you'd care to tell me just what you are doing inside Miss Esther and Miss Louise's home when I know for a fact they have gone for the day and aren't here right now?" We looked over to the front door at the police officer who had just asked us that question. Before we could reply, the sound of soft footfalls on the stairs had us spinning, only to watch incredulously as an elderly lady made her way gracefully down the steps and smiling, stopped in front of us.

"No need to worry, Officer Wilkins. These are my guests."

"Oh! Pardon, Miss Millicent. I didn't know you were home, or I would have kept on driving by. When I saw these folks spread out all over the place I came to worry."

"Indeed. I'd expect nothing less." Millicent nodded and led the man back to the entry, where she bade him farewell then firmly shut the door behind him. Turning to us, she smiled then said, "Now...what can I do to get the lot of you to leave me in peace?"

* * *

THE NEXT THIRTY minutes were bizarre, if I may say so—and I did.

"I'm telling you, Esther and Louise showed up in my tent carrying a lamp they insisted carried your deceased spirit." I perched at the end of a chair in the living room where Millicent held court surrounded by my team. "You certainly don't look dead!"

Considering none of us could pull much of a reading off this woman, we had to play this as straight human interaction since we couldn't be sure if she had some paranormal ability. We've never had this happen to us—at least one team member could determine if we were dealing with a witch, a vampire, etc. To have not one of us signal that the woman before us was one of us was problematic and had me highly troubled. Even Serena and Sydney looked puzzled.

For her part, Millicent was playing her cards close and

remained serene and a tad condescending. She was imposing in stature and must have been at least five foot eleven in her sensible flats. Her hair streaked with grey still showed much of her dark locks, and she wore it up in a loose bun. Her eyes were a bewitching hazel and clear for a woman supposedly in her early eighties. Her skin tone didn't differ that much from ours. Johnny was darker, but he always sported a tan even throughout the winter months with his gorgeous Italian good looks. Bella was darker and Antoine darker still since he's Black. Millicent even had a smattering of freckles. The two sisters made her sound like a rare and exotic creature when she first arrived in their home. However, while striking in looks, she didn't look like someone who would have stood out years ago in a world that was much different and less tolerant than today.

"And you rushed right over and with a key! I'm assuming you are amateur ghost hunters of some sort. You don't look like thieves. My sisters are very dear to me, but I'm afraid they have great flights of fancy take over from time to time. I fear their age is catching up to them."

"They said they found you dead and then your body vanished. Then claimed you wound up in that lamp on the library desk, possessing it so you didn't have to be buried," Dara stated.

"And yet, here I am." Millicent smiled serenely.

"Where are they? Your sisters?" I asked.

"Alas, they are being evaluated back at the doctor's office. He was rather displeased with their lab work results, and I fear they may need to be in an assisted living facility." Millicent proclaimed this with a slight smile on her face. I decided I didn't like her attitude much. I liked it even less when she held her hand out for the house key. "I've just mastered learning how to maneuver around a laptop and the internet and have been busy researching facilities close to my home.

This way, I could drop in or plan a visit without it being too much of an inconvenience to me."

"That's rather convenient, don't you think? I mean, yesterday they were sound enough to show up at our appraisal caravan seeking aid, and suddenly, today they are too feebleminded to be on their own taking care of their affairs?" Nathara chided. That's the thing about Nathara that made me able to tolerate her moodiness. When she knows an injustice is occurring or some mischief is afoot of the evil variety, she is all in to rectify the situation.

"Convenient? No. It won't be easy for me to manage this house alone, not that they were much help in recent years. But they will be better off if the doctor agrees they need to be cared for in a home."

"Who took them? Surely, they didn't go off on their own if they are as fragile as you suggest?" Dara asked.

"Of course not! They have a lovely nurse that I've employed for the last few years who does a fantastic job with the two dears but cannot handle them as they've become much more difficult to maintain, what with these delusions and going off on their own. Now, I'm busy. There is much to be done today and while I appreciate you checking into their well-being, I must bring this little meeting to a close." Millicent stood, as did much of my group.

"This house is very grand. I can see how difficult it must be for one person to maintain. Do you not have help?" Antoine queried.

Millicent paused before responding and gave him an enigmatic look, almost flirtatious, before she said, "Of course. One cannot manage this vast a home without having caretakers and maids. We even employ a cook. It is very grand and very old and requires round-the-clock care at times. I wish there were strong men around here to help with the heavy stuff."

"Do they ever mention odd noises or strange goings-on?" I asked Millicent, who turned to me with a frown that she quickly removed from her face. "The help? Do they hear things?"

"What an extraordinary question. So curious. It's an old house. I'm sure it creaks and groans from time to time. However, I haven't heard any such thing. But then again, I am older and my hearing isn't what it used to be, I'm sure. Now, I regret you had to come out of your way for such nonsense, but I am very busy so I must bid you farewell."

Millicent escorted us back to the front door and shut it firmly once we had crossed the threshold onto the porch.

"Well, I guess that's that," Dara stated.

"I wouldn't be so sure," I responded and watched in amusement as everyone turned their heads to me in tandem.

"Why do you say that Mags? Is there something we missed?" Sven asked.

I turned to Ellie, who just materialized back on this side of the door. She came from her position inside the foyer—a place she was forbidden from entering but had obviously disregarded in her impatience. Apparently, easily surpassed by her curiosity, she ignored waiting for us to signal that the coast was clear and that she could safely enter.

"That woman knows something. It's something that has to do with our world, and I can prove it," I replied, gazing back at the door in speculation. "You see, just as we were leaving, I happened to notice Ellie here floating by the grand staircase in the foyer."

"What does that have to do with anything?" Nathara grumbled.

"Well, I'd stake my life on it that Millicent noticed Ellie as well if the look on her face was any indication before she hid her surprise."

That news caused everyone to glance back at the grand

gothic Victorian as we stood by our vehicles. A slight move-ment of the curtain on the upper floor indicated Millicent or someone else noticed the pause in our departure.

I had a feeling we would be sticking around these parts despite the main antique convoy moving on in two days' time. How could we possibly leave with such an intriguing case on our hands? Because one thing is for sure, something is going on in that house, and I intended to find out what kind of evil we were dealing with, and I meant to do it quickly.

CHAPTER 6

I spent the evening in my RV with Ellie pouring over folklore, spellcasting, and other books I had in my possession dealing with the outré. We only had a few customers before we closed for the evening, and I was grateful it was a light load because mentally, I was fried.

Bob sat between Ellie and me on the floor, occasionally pawing at the bookmark I used to mark my place—its tassel tempting him into action.

"What do you think is going on at that place?" Ellie asked, rubbing my shoulder in sympathy.

Unlike most ghosts, for some reason that I didn't have the answer for, Ellie and I were able to touch. I could feel her skin; my hand didn't go through her. She was also rather adept at moving obstacles, and it bolstered my suspicions that she might not be fully in the ghostly realm but suspended in between by some erratic form of magic. I know it shocked our cousin, Lily, which was the catalyst that prompted her to promise to help us figure out the phenomena at a later date.

"We could be dealing with an illusion of some sort. Or a

powerfully evil woman. Or even an entity that is manipulating things without Millicent nor the two Birch sisters being aware." I worried my bottom lip then continued.

"What I don't like is not knowing what happened to Esther and Louise. Are they back home? Did the doctor admit them to an assisted living facility? How long would that take if he or she did anyway? I need more info to verify whether Millicent was lying to us and is the evil one we need to tackle, or if the elder two sisters are a tad senile and Millicent is innocent."

"She is creepy," Ellie avowed, and I couldn't disagree with her—Millicent *was* creepy!

"I know what I saw—and heard. I'm trying to look up what kind of manifestation appears faceless and keens. We aren't dealing with a banshee or poltergeist. Unfortunately, they are fairly easy to take out," I complained.

"You need to look into Millicent's past."

I looked up as Bella entered the RV and engaged me after overhearing what I'd been saying.

Ellie waved at her and asked, "Why?" Although I could hear her ask the question, Bella had to read her lips. "Because Maggie here, told us of Millicent's adoption by Mr. Birch. Millicent was the daughter of his exotic wife who came from the Caribbean. That nugget of information is screaming that magic might be at play from West Africa and or the native tribes who lived on those islands. It may even suggest a mix of European trickery and enchantment tossed in for good measure."

"That is a great idea, Bella and you are about thirty minutes too late," I stated, holding up the book I'd been perusing. "I've already grabbed a book on religions, cults, and folk traditions from around the world and planned on a little light voodoo reading this evening." I smiled as she nodded with pleasure that I'd already thought to go that route.

"That's not the only thing my dear sister has planned," Ellie carefully enunciated so Bella could follow.

Bella turned to me and raised one brow. "Oh?"

I sighed inwardly and smiled instead of explaining.

"You plan on sneaking back over there tonight and breaking in, aren't you?" Bella guessed.

"Bella. You can't sound the alarm. I can't show up with a posse, and you know it. This is going to require some stealth."

"You are going to need someone to watch your back. I'm coming with you."

"No, you are not."

"Yes, I am. Or I will tell Antoine."

"What is this? Third grade?" I grumbled giving Bella a hard stare.

It didn't faze her in the slightest and she popped a bubble as her only response. We all stood there for a moment and the only sound was Bella chewing her gum loudly and popping even more bubbles.

"Fine. You can come."

Bella began clapping her hands and looked victorious.

"Yay! I didn't need your permission for your information. But thanks anyway!" She gave me a cheesy grin and sat down on my sofa. "Now, how do you plan on getting into the house?"

"Easy. I had Sven make me another key before we left this morning, and I'm glad I did. I wanted to smack that woman when she held her hand out quietly demanding the key back. She is up to something, and I hope it doesn't mean the two sisters are in danger."

Ellie flapped her hands to get Bella's attention.

"You better dress in dark clothing and conceal some weapons on your persons—the mundane and the magical. I don't like the idea of you heading back there without more backup," Ellie fussed.

"You mean men. Big beefy men, so they can save us when we get into distress." Bella barked out a laugh.

"I do not!" Ellie chided.

"Yes, she does," I responded, poking a bit of fun at my sibling. "Ellie just loves it when a big, strong hunk of man comes rushing in to save the day. She spends all her waking hours reading those ridiculous romance novels."

"Considering I never sleep I have plenty of time to read— and not all of them are romance. Thank you very much!" she sniffed.

* * *

IN THE WEE hours that next morning, Bella and I crept out of my RV and quietly made our way over to my vehicle. I opened the door and gently closed it. Turning over the engine, I paused to see if the noise would bring out any curious looky-loo's, but when all remained dark I put the vehicle in drive.

I didn't turn on my headlights until we cleared the parking lot and turned right onto the highway that led out of town and to the next town where the sisters lived. I made sure to keep within the speed limit and slowly made my way back along the same route we had taken the previous morning.

"I'm going to park around the corner from the Birch home, and we will walk through the neighbor's yard into their backyard and do a bit of recognizance before we break in. I hope the household is asleep and they are all heavy sleepers, or this will turn into a nightmare fast," I told Bella and she nodded in agreement.

We parked and stealthily made our way around the

neighbor's house and came to a brief halt when we hit a fence.

"Here's hoping they don't have any dogs," Bella whispered.

We opened the latch and crept into the backyard. From my vantage point, I could see we were one house over from the Birch home and would need to hop the back fence, turn left, and hightail it over the sisters' fence and into their backyard. I breathed a sigh of relief when no sound of dogs barking started as we made our way to the next obstacle.

"No worries. If they did, I would have just frozen them in place," Bella whisper-giggled.

I blinked. I loved animals and was afraid to ask the elemental if she meant freezing them permanently, or like they'd thaw after ten minutes or so. I didn't think I wanted to hear her answer.

When we were finally in the Birch garden, concealed behind two massive magnolia trees, we paused to scrutinize the windows and back porch and both of us were startled when a light turned on in a downstairs room.

"This can't be good," I whispered to Bella. She nodded and made a "shh" motion with her finger to her lips.

Creeping ever so gently across the lawn, we stood bent into a crouch just beneath the illuminated window. Bella made an up motion, indicating she'd take a peek and I gave her the thumbs up. I waited while she positioned herself to best hide from detection then watched as she carefully rose enough to spy through the windowpane. Noticing a shimmering glow encircle her, I wondered at the magic Bella was employing. I could hear a soft buzzing sound and then all was silent again.

I heard a quick intake of breath and almost toppled over when Bella quickly squatted once more, eyes wide and her hand over her mouth in shock. I looked deep into her eyes and noticed they'd changed color with tiny flames dancing in her irises. Whoa.

"What? Did you see someone?" I barely breathed out the question.

Bella's head bobbed up and down, and she grabbed my arm, pulling me back across the yard where we hid under the branches of one of the magnolias.

"There is a dead body laid out in the room I just looked in. A fairly fresh one too. And I could see the light across the hall and noticed an open door which looks to be the kitchen beyond. But there is a dead man. He is *not* sleeping, in that room!"

"Why do you say dead? I mean, he *could* be asleep."

Bella chewed at her bottom lip, glancing back at the house.

"Sweetie, I know dead. I sniffed for a soul and didn't find one. Plus, explain to me why he has crossed arms, hands resting on his chest and he's tinted a weird shade of bluish grey?"

Oh, well, if we were going to split hairs and all that.

Wait. Sniff?

"What do we do now?" I wondered aloud.

"I think we need to get in there and find out what's going on... but we need someone who can get in and out without detection and can eavesdrop with ease."

"Yeah, but I left Ellie back at the fairgrounds. Plus, I wouldn't put her in danger of a ghostly attack or some other dark magic. Especially since we don't know what we are up against yet."

"Well, you aren't going to be pleased with what I'm about to say then."

I peered at Bella and watched as her eyes flickered over to the house, then back at me, giving me an apologetic grimace.

"What? What's wrong?"

"Ellie was standing next to the dead guy and gave me a little salute just now. I guess she followed us here."

"What?! I am going to kill her! Um, argh! Forget I said that."

Groan.

I would have wrung her neck had she still been among the living. As it now stood, she was our only chance of discovering what was going on in that place. And we all knew it.

I felt the onset of a massive headache coming. This was not going to go down well at all. Why would it?

CHAPTER 7

Twenty minutes went by, and the only sign that something had occurred was the light going out in the room with the body and Ellie in it. Nothing moved. No sign of life—obviously. Everything was quiet.

"We have to get in there," I said.

"We are going to have to figure out the best way in."

"Yeah. I wish Ellie would help us out here. But she is probably mad at us for leaving her behind. I didn't see her tag along and that means she's learned how to fade out and avoid detection."

"Which infers she could be standing right beside us listening in," Bella responded drolly.

The two of us began looking around as if we expected to find Ellie floating nearby, and after a few sheepish minutes, realizing we probably looked like idiots, we stopped and crept back over to the window.

"That was pretty stupid."

"Yeah. I really am going to throttle her, though. If I can catch her."

Bella snickered and peered into the window again. Then

she stood up with the look of incredulity on her face. Following suit, I stood up and looked in the window to see what brought about such puzzlement then felt my mouth drop open.

"The body is gone!" I hastened to point out in a hushed whisper.

"And Esther and Louise are back and sitting on the sofa in the dark. Do you think they are dead too?" Bella began to sniff. This was getting weird.

"I don't know what to think."

Creepy! Creepy was what I was thinking. What the hell were those two ladies up to?

Glancing to my right, I made a hasty decision to climb onto the back porch and check the obvious—try the back door to see if anyone locked it. Gently turning the knob, I was surprised when the door opened with barely a squeak. I sent a quick prayer up to the makers of WD-40 and pushed the door open the rest of the way. Pausing to see if we caught the notice of anyone present, I peered back to make sure Bella was behind me then signaled for her to close the door once we were in.

Ever so slowly, we made our way into the room where Esther and Louise sat, hands folded on their laps. Their eyes were closed, and I couldn't tell if they were breathing or not —yet. Bella kneeled in front of Esther and gently reached her hand out to touch her. That's when both of their eyes flew open at the same time, and they began to shout. Louise even went so far as to hurl a toss pillow at my head and kick out her legs. All this managed to do was cause her to slide forward and off the sofa, onto the floor, and land in a heap.

"Oof! Esther! Quick. Grab your gun! Intruders! Help! They are going to kill us in our sleep!"

"We aren't sleeping any longer, sister. And how do you expect me to reach my gun with these two standing in the way? Oh! It's you!" Esther peered up at me with her tiny bird-like eyes and smiled. "Calm yourself, Louise, and please get up off the floor. You look like a ninny!"

I quickly helped the older woman back onto the sofa and began to apologize for startling the two of them awake.

Bella had the sense to reach over and turn on the lamp on the end table beside the sofa lighting the room in a soft glow. I paused momentarily to take in what was a room that time forgot. In keeping with the Victorian style, the entire room was an homage to the era with intricate wallpaper and period furnishings. The relatively large room was ornately stuffy, yet at the same time, it was charming and quaint and right out of an old movie.

I expected our little commotion would have Millicent running—or gracefully rushing to see the cause, but I heard no other sounds in the house. I wondered about the servants, thinking it odd that only the two old ladies acknowledged our presence.

"Are you OK? We were worried about you, especially since Millicent informed us you were at the doctor yesterday. She mentioned something about the possibility of you going to someplace where you could both be looked after?" I asked.

Esther and Louise glanced at each other then back at me.

"You must be mistaken, my dear. We only went out shopping then stopped in at the doctor to pick up a prescription so we could renew our handicap tag for my car," Esther informed us. "How did you manage to communicate with Millicent? Did you speak to the lamp she's hiding in?"

I blinked.

Bella snorted and crossed her arms, giving me a look that asked, *now what?*

I shrugged and turned back to the sisters.

"Ladies, I am not sure what is going on, but yesterday

when we came over with our team, Millicent came waltzing down the steps after a concerned police officer stopped in to see what we were doing in your home."

"Oh! But that's impossible, dear. Millicent is dead!" Louise insisted.

My patience was running thin, and I had other things to deal with—a possible body—not to mention a missing ghost of a sister. Not bothering to give the ladies another second of this, this—*whatever* this was, I pulled out my phone and called Antoine.

It was time to call in the troops.

Again.

* * *

"NICE OF YOU TO decide to take off and not tell anyone your plans. I'd like to put in my vote that she be brought up on some kind of disciplinary action. Or just get flogged until she cries like a baby," Nathara drawled as she walked in the back door.

I suggested to Antoine that he pull in the Birch drive and park around back, so we didn't have a repeat with any do-gooding, roving police officers. I'm sure the neighborhood watch would alert the authorities if ten people, most of them dressed in black, were seen entering the front door en masse.

For their part, Esther and Louise managed to stay out of our way, content to sit and sip tea in the formal dining room while we tore apart their home, albeit neatly. My team had witnessed Millicent greeting the officer who seemed to believe she was a living, breathing entity, so we either had to prove she was still among the living and the sisters *were* senile or set off some kind of trigger to bring her ghost out to play. All that and find out what the heck happened to Ellie—which had me beyond distracted with worry. Not a good thing to be when dealing with possible malevolence.

Serena and Sydney began systematically going from room to room and clearing them, with Bella and Sven tagging along. Dara set up Madame Myna on the table next to Esther and Louise and began chanting at the crystal ball, running her hand over and around it. Johnny and Tor started checking the rooms for a more mundane explanation for the recent events and looked for the human element and any trickery they could find. Nathara was going around the house casting reveal spells, trying to find the supernatural, which left Antoine and me alone in the parlor where the body laid just an hour ago now.

Was it only an hour?

"Tell me again what you saw in here." Antoine was crawling all around the upholstered bench where Bella said the body was. He was looking for something—anything to verify a dead person was ever there. "I can't be one hundred percent certain, but there does seem to be a trace of something here." Antoine wrinkled his nose in disgust as if his keen vampire olfactory abilities caught something unpleasant in the fabric.

"What? Like, you can smell death?"

Ew. I wouldn't like that superpower. What is it with some members of the team and sniffing for souls—or...

Instead of answering me, Antoine whipped out his cell phone and called Johnny. Our werewolf was with us in a matter of minutes and began scenting the area around the bench.

I know. Weirdness, everywhere.

"There was a body here most definitely," Johnny informed us then turned his head in the direction of the front of the house. "I think the trail leads back that way, so if we follow it..."

Whatever he was going to say was cut short when the unmistakable sound of the doorbell stopped everyone in their tracks.

Not again.

Yes again.

By the time we arrived in the foyer, Louise had opened the door and ushered Officer Wilkins—I caught his name this time—back in. However, his partner, Officer Anand, accompanied him, so now we had two of them to deal with. Both men looked around suspiciously and when their eyes found mine and Antoine's, they narrowed. Yes, because an unusually tall Black man with incredible blue eyes and a flaming redhead dressed head to toe like a ninja was something you'd find hanging around the gothic Victorian home of two elderly Southern ladies in Tennessee at two in the morning.

At least now we might discover if Millicent was still among the living and the Birch sisters were senile nonagenarians.

"Officers! So nice to see you." Esther came creeping into the foyer, beaming at the two men.

"Miss Louise. Miss Esther. We were getting off patrol and got a call from a neighbor telling us the lights have been turning on and off all over your home. And why am I not surprised to see you people back here? Are you sure you ladies know these characters? Nothing bad is going on here, right?"

Characters?

Esther and Louise tittered and flapped their hands in amusement like two marionettes in the hands of a puppet master, so alike was their response.

"Oh no. We know you are doing your duty, gentlemen, but this is the lady we hired to look into some things for us.

They are antique appraisers, and we brought a few items for them to evaluate."

"At this hour?" Officer Anand raised his eyebrows in disbelief.

"Oh, you know how it is when you get to our age. We never sleep at regular times. This lovely young lady is from a well-known family of appraisers. We did our research, Officer Anand. We couldn't be in better hands."

An unreadable look passed between the two officers that didn't make me feel they believed Esther's explanation.

Officer Wilkins turned to me but continued to query the two sisters. "But ladies, how do you know they aren't here casing your home—a house filled with priceless antiques and that they don't intend to take advantage of you? I find it highly suspicious that an entire brigade of antique appraisers descends upon this place at such a late hour without having an ulterior motive."

"My dear man. We are perfectly capable of judging the character of someone we've hired. You needn't worry about us." Esther patted the officer on the arm and clucked a little to show her dismay at his assumptions.

"But this late, or early rather?" Officer Anand wouldn't let it alone it seemed.

"We were going to have a late-night anyway, Officer Anand. Sister and I were preparing one of our gentlemen for burial, and it was the perfect time for this group to head over without disrupting their schedules for tomorrow."

I know my mouth dropped open when I heard what Esther had said, but the two police officers remained utterly unphased by the mention of gentlemen needing planting. Antoine's eyes went positively wide open in shock. I've never seen him this rattled before. Our collective astonishment must have convinced the two men that we were innocent of any wrongdoing, or at least were nonplussed with the revelation we'd just heard.

Another look passed between the men, and I had a feeling things were about to go south. I just didn't realize how *far* south it would actually be.

CHAPTER 8

*T*he next half hour turned into a scavenger hunt of sorts with both officers going from room to room looking for something—we just were not sure what.

This was because Officer Wilkins informed me that Louise and Esther had a bit of lapse in their memory and on occasion, still believed they were the town's undertakers. The back parlor was where they would have their 'customers' lie in state. No wonder it looked like something out of a Hitchcock film.

The Birch sisters failed to mention their previous profession, which would explain the scent of death that permeated the parlor—but it didn't explain the body Bella spied through the window nor what had happened to it.

"Perhaps what Bella saw was a vision from the past. They sometimes manifest like ghosts in these old homes. I only wish Ellie would return and let us know what she'd discovered," Antoine whispered to me while we watched the officers methodically search the rooms. They kept throwing us suspicious glances that were getting on my nerves. I am one of those people who respect the police but can't help getting nervous around them, especially while driving. If I was out and about running errands and a cop car pulled up behind me, I went all freak out stupid in my head.

I don't know why! I was the angel in the family. Ellie was the one out joyriding as a teen and running amok with her friends.

I nodded to Antoine, acknowledging his theory, but I knew I had to get up and move or I'd start sweating like a convict on death row on the morning of his 'Big Day.'

I shot up and began walking to the foyer then into the library. I stared at the stupid lamp and wondered if the two officers would find Millicent upstairs in one of the many bedrooms, asleep with a sleeping mask over her eyes, and startle her to death when they entered unannounced in her room.

Now convinced the two sisters were indeed feebleminded and the keening was probably old ghosts from the past, which wasn't unusual in a house this old, I wanted this over. A few simple spooks could be dealt with quickly, and we could move on to the next town with a clear conscience. Millicent could deal with her confounded siblings without our aid.

Plus, Bella and her soul sniffing, had insisted she'd not gotten a dead reading off Millicent either. What was going on around here?

I wandered over to the desk and pulled the chain on the lamp. It turned on and I shrugged. No howling banshee. Nothing out of the ordinary. Sighing, I glanced at the bookshelves and only then did I notice the overabundance of tomes on the mortuary arts.

Creepy.

I turned and walked back over to the window seat where I'd seen the shrieking woman and lifted the lid, fully expecting to find an empty bench like before.

Instead, I found the body of a dead man staring up at me. That's when I heard someone clear their throat behind me.

"What have we here?"

"Aaah!" I dropped the lid and spun around at the sound of Officer Anand's voice then promptly sat on the window seat and planted my hands on either side of me.

"What? Nothing! What would I have? I've never been in this room before. I was just killing time..." Perhaps not the best choice of words all things considered.

Eyes narrowing again in mistrust, I could tell the man was about to go all cop on me, and I blurted out another doozy.

"It's not like there's a body in the window seat or anything!"

I did *not* just say that.

From the look on the man's face, I most assuredly had indeed, uttered those damning words. What on earth was wrong with me?

I mentally slapped myself on the head.

"There you are!" Nathara came slithering into the room, and I watched in amazement as Officer Anand's eyes glazed over and a look of wonder crossed his face.

Did I mention how gorgeous Nathara was? I hated the woman, but she did come in handy in situations such as these—and in our line of work, we had them more often than you might think.

"You, uh, you were looking for me?" Officer Anand asked in amazement at his good luck.

"Of course, I was. Silly man. Aren't you just delightful? Louise asked me to find you and bring you to the kitchen. She put on a pot of coffee and wanted to offer you a cup. Come. Take my hand, and we can go find her. Shall we?"

Like a lamb to the slaughter, Officer Anand obeyed the

deceitful vixen and I found myself ignored and forgotten but still quaking from my near miss.

Nathara gave me a penetrating gaze as if trying to impart some message in departure, but as I hadn't a clue what she might mean by it, I decided to stay right where I was and called Antoine on my phone.

"We have a situation."

"Oh, you think?"

"No. A real situation. Like, a real, *real* situation. Get in here, quick."

"Mags..."

"There is a freakin' body in the window seat, Antoine. Get. In. Here. Now!" I rasped out the words in a fierce murmur, and the silence that met me spoke volumes.

"I'll be right there."

Of course, you will.

What followed was right out of that Cary Grant movie which was eerily similar to our circumstances.

Nathara played Mata Hari in the kitchen, keeping both officers captivated by her sweet nothings and coquettish allure.

While that little drama was playing out, Dara had to sneak Madame Myna back into her vast tote bag and brought both Birch sisters into the room where we first saw the dead body to have a little chat. Bella went with them.

Johnny and Tor decided to wander the perimeter of the house, keeping an eye out for Millicent and Ellie—after all, my sister had to be somewhere around here. And at this point, I wondered if Millicent was a specter and they were having tea together or something.

I had no idea where Sydney and Serena were. The entire house was still, and they never came down when the door-bell had rung earlier. I only hoped, wherever they were hiding out, they managed to find out answers. This was quickly turning into a farce.

That was partially due to Antoine, Sven, and I trying to decide what to do about the dead guy.

Not only was he dead. He was stiff. Which means he was, *ahem*, freshly dead, as Bella inferred. Or at least still in the twelve hours following a death in which a body stayed in that condition. This was going to make moving him beyond difficult.

How the heck did this man come to be a goner, in rigor, straight as a board with arms crossed. Did he die lying on that bench? I mean, was he dead, and the Birch sisters stretched him out and placed his hands in a crossed position on his chest and *then* rigor mortis set in? I can't imagine he'd just walked in the back room, decided to die, and put himself in a funerary position knowing he'd turn into a stiffy within two hours!

"Where are we going to put him?"

"I'm more puzzled about how we will manage to get him up and out as stiff as he is. This is going to be difficult," Sven complained, glancing over his shoulder toward the formal rooms.

"We have to get him out of here and down into the basement. Officer Wilkins had just come up from searching there when you called," Antoine informed me.

"Well, that's great, but we have one little problem. The cops are in the kitchen where the basement door is."

Sven walked around the desk and back into the foyer. I followed and watched as he blended into the wall disappearing from sight. I rejoined Antoine and waited. After a few more seconds, Sven came back into the library.

"There is another door in the foyer that I thought was another coat closet. It isn't. It's a butler's pantry and it leads into the kitchen. If we can get the cops out of there and have

Nathara move them into the living room, and if we time it right, we can take this guy through the butler pantry and down to the basement, then head back here and play like we've been waiting around."

"How do we tell Nathara our plan?" I wondered aloud.

Antoine held up his phone then began texting.

"Don't tell her outright what we are doing! Just let her know we need her in the living room!" I blurted quickly.

Antoine raised his eyebrows. "Oh, you think?"

Fine. He knows what to do. I know he knows. But cops, me, my weird disorder where I lose brain cells around them. I was on edge!

"Quick. I didn't tell her anything except to move to the dining room leisurely and give us a moment, then continue into the living room, but not too far in to see the foyer, and hit delete now. Then I sent another text, and asked her if she remembered where I put my sunglasses."

Smart move. Nathara would get the text, read the first part then see our code for immediate-erase mode, which was the delete mention. This way, if the cops reacted to her getting a text, they'd only see Antoine asking about his glasses.

"Maggie, stay here in case they come through. You were present and should remain. This way, it looks like you have nothing to hide. Sven and I will take our friend here for a nice little walk."

I was about to argue but realized Antoine was right. If Officer Anand came back and saw me sitting on the window seat, he might assume I never left, and I could try and buy the guys more time.

I watched in fascination as the two men lifted the stiff up and out of the window seat, which, on the way back down, suddenly decided to creak and groan like it hadn't been oiled in years. We looked at each other in abject horror, then the guys hotfooted it into the foyer, and I lost sight of them. I anticipated they'd made it into the butler's pantry since I could already hear Nathara laughing at something one of the officers said and prayed she'd be able to maintain their attention.

Suddenly all sound stopped. The entire house got eerily quiet. I waited another minute but my curiosity got the better of me, and I crept into the foyer. I was about to peek in the butler's pantry when Officer Anand rushed up behind me.

"What are you doing?"

"Eek! What is wrong with you? I was just looking for everyone because I got bored and thought maybe you needed to speak with me again."

The man was giving me a *yeah right* face then seemed to notice the door. He went on high alert, and I groaned inwardly, knowing we were about to have all hell break loose if the guys hadn't gotten the body down to the basement.

"What do we have here?" The officer pushed his way into the butler's pantry and continued into the kitchen. He radioed to his partner, and Officer Wilkins came in from the formal rooms in a hurry, Nathara on his heels.

"What's up?"

"What's up is I find this woman sneaking into the kitchen from the foyer, and that big guy is nowhere to be found. Now isn't that interesting since he headed out of here not fifteen minutes ago after she called him on his cell?"

Both officers turned to look at me and I played dumb. I think I came by it honestly in this situation, and I'm sure I looked like a dunderhead, but it didn't seem to convince either of them I was innocent. I was about to suggest we inspect the window seat when we heard the most unbeliev-able racket coming from above us. Our eyes locked on the ceiling in wonder. It sounded like something bumping and crashing into the walls, then ended with a loud *thunk* and a groan before all became silent again.

"What the hell was that?" Officer Wilkins looked like a man who had just about had enough of the hijinks going on around here, and not even the allure of Nathara could stop him from investigating.

When I was in the kitchen earlier, I failed to notice a back staircase which must have been how the servants went to the upper floors back in the day—or present-day for all I knew.

Just as both officers went to open the basement door and catch my two friends, Serena and Sydney came tumbling into the kitchen from the staircase, looking all sleepy-eyed and tussled. I don't mean they looked terrible or unattractive, just the opposite. They appeared as two angels after a sublime night of slumber in their lovers' arms. If I thought Nathara had the two men bewitched, the sight of our two succubi had the cops turning to a puddle of goo. All it took was for Serena to stumble a little and giggle-fall into Officer Wilkin's arms while Sydney pretended to feel faint, slipping slightly, before the quick-thinking Officer Anand reached out to steady her.

"Oh, thank you so. We've been up in the attic going through a trunk. Louise informed us it had old tablecloths from the fifties. I just love textiles. Don't you?"

Serena nodded like she was supposed to answer, then turned to Officer Wilkins and gave a soft smile. "Thank you for catching me. The air up in that attic is so stuffy. I feel like I can't catch my breath."

She then proceeded to take deep breaths in and out while her chest rose and fell to the occasion. That was all it took to enchant the men, making them putty in her hands.

"Please, maybe a glass of water? And can we go sit a spell in the living room? I believe it is cooler in there."

I can't tell you how quickly they forgot me in their haste

to get glasses of water and a soft cushioned sofa seat for the two blondes. Even Nathara was left in the dust.

The minute the cops were gone, Nathara spun around and gave me a look like *where the heck are they?* I shrugged but pointed to the basement steps and tiptoed over to the door. Just as I was about to open it, Antoine pushed it open and missed my nose by mere inches.

"Whoa! Hey. Where did they go?" he asked quietly.

"Succubi," I whispered back.

A brief moment of relief crossed his face then his demeanor immediately switched back to concerned, and he informed me we had another situation. "What now? What could be worse than this?"

"Sven is stuck in the dumbwaiter with the body."

Wait. What?

CHAPTER 9

"*How* ow? What? When did you...?"

Another hour had passed, and thankfully it was without our two men of law and order. Esther and Louise insisted that the two officers return to their families, get some sleep, and leave their stellar antique appraisers in peace. A phone call from their lieutenant played a big part in convincing the duo of our innocence. Esther pulled some strings and name-dropped. The Fortune good name must have saved us because I could hear the man barking orders to retreat from the kitchen as the officers rushed out into the early morning air.

I had a million questions for our elderly patrons, but that had to wait since we had to free Sven from his upright prison. Unfortunately, he was wedged in tight and in a too familiar position with our stiff. They were practically nose-to-nose in the dumbwaiter chute which had come crashing down to settle in the basement. This was the cacophony we'd heard earlier.

"I still don't understand why you went up when we'd planned on you heading down. And why the dumbwaiter?"

"It hasn't been used in years! My word! But I am sure it is rusted through, and that's what caused it to give way," Louise proclaimed.

Oh, do you think?

"We couldn't, uh, fit him down the stairs. They are narrow and he's—um—stiff." Antoine looked uncomfortable at his error in judgment and was awaiting on an explanation from the two sisters. Heck, we all were. But right now, we had more pressing matters to deal with. Sven could not possibly be comfortable in that tiny space!

"Why isn't he shifting? Sven? He can shift! Why isn't he so that the body will drop, and he can free himself?

"Mags, he is traumatized right now with the dead guy's nose in his neck. I tried to convince him to give way and shift out of there, but he's not thinking clearly. He said something about confined spaces, and I do believe our shifter is claustrophobic," Antoine intoned dejectedly.

"Hang on. I know Sven is our priority here, but I have to know. Is Millicent really dead, or are you ladies taking us for a ride here?" Nathara demanded. "And what's with the dead man? Are you responsible for that?"

Dara tsked and shook her head. She too wanted answers. Being a druid and a cleric, she wanted the body tended to in a timely manner. And since there wasn't much the elderly duo could do to help Sven, they could talk while we worked on freeing him.

"How did you manage to move him from the back parlor and into the window seat is what I'd like to know!" she added.

"Millicent is evil. Always has been, always will be, even in death. Please. You must believe us! She is doing some kind of hocus-pocus magic from the islands. If you saw her here yesterday as you claim, it must mean she can manifest and appear human. She even fooled that nice Officer Wilkins," Esther wailed.

"Evil!" Madame Myna chose that moment to wail out a prediction of doom. She often waited until someone else made a similar prophecy. Not that she wasn't adept in her foresight. She just liked backup.

"George isn't our fault," cried Louise. "He knew better than to sample Father's elixirs, especially after so many decades! We warned him. Why didn't he listen?"

George? Was he the dead man? I would have said something in reply but suddenly found my mouth as dry as the Sahara when Tor stood upright and whipped off his sweater then tossed it onto a workbench nearby. I knew it was stuffy in the tight quarters we were inhabiting and didn't blame him for trying to stay cool, but no man had the right to look that good shirtless. It was obscene how perfect a specimen he was. Rippling muscles and broad-shouldered perfection, even his hair came loose in the struggle and cascaded down his back. I felt the onset of drool with all the saliva that suddenly flooded my mouth.

"Ahem!"

Nathara caught my eye and smirked knowingly. The witch.

I tore my eyes away from the perfect V-shaped back and addressed Esther. "What proof do you have that Millicent has dabbled with island magic? Do you mean voodoo? Why didn't you tell me this when we first met?"

I saw Johnny remove his sweater and toss it over near Tor's, but I didn't feel compelled to stop what I was doing to stare at *his* torso. Man, was I in trouble. A lightbulb went off in my head, and I stopped everything and made myself look at Johnny in the hopes it would fool Nathara into thinking I would watch any guy showing off his body. No such luck, however, because she snickered at my feeble attempt.

"Nice try," Nathara said under her breath, quietly enough that I am sure I was the only one who heard.

"Try shoving him upward while you wiggle downward," Johnny was yelling up the chute.

We could hear Sven's reply, and it wasn't something I care to repeat.

"Well, I'm sorry you will have to get over having his crotch in your face, man. I can't think of any other way to nudge him out of your way!" Johnny ran a hand through his hair in frustration while looking around the room for something to give him leverage.

Antoine had gone from barking instructions to stomping up the tenuous structure that I hesitated to call steps now that I could see just how flimsy they were. He went into the kitchen, where I heard him continue up the back staircase. Suddenly, the dust began pooling down the chute with bits of plaster and other unidentified pieces.

Grunting sounds intensified, and we held our collective breaths until we heard a shout of warning then watched in fascination as the lower half of the dead man came crashing down the chute with a bang. Tor and Johnny began to wrestle his stiff body out of the tiny opening and managed to free the corpse after about ten minutes of finagling him around—I won't say we didn't hear a few snap, crackles, and pops in the process.

Once George was free from his upright prison, the men laid him down on a worktable in one corner of the basement.

Sven came staggering through the wall having finally shifted and he looked like a train wreck. He immediately pulled out a pack of cigarettes and strode up the steps and disappeared. I assumed he went straight out the front door and was currently sucking in gobs off his toxic stick. I guess he really did have a problem with confined spaces.

And dead bodies being pressed up close and personal.

"Now, what do we do with him?" Tor asked no one in particular.

"Now we toss him in the retort," Louise suggested with a bland smile.

"Retort?"

"The cremation chamber...furnace. Behind you, dear."

We all turned to where Louise pointed and found ourselves looking at a conspicuous, shiny structure that stated it was from the American Crematory Equipment company, model A-250. How the hell did they manage to get that thing down here and how had we missed it?

"Ladies, I was under the assumption you two are now retired. Why do you have a working crematory in your basement?"

"We still do the occasional body for friends of the family and relations. Our business has been here for decades. We opened the funeral home when we were in our twenties, right after we graduated from mortuary school. We've been taking care of the deceased loved ones of this town since the 1950s!" Esther bragged. She even pressed the button to give us a glance inside the chamber. It was dark and slightly dusty and looked like it hadn't been properly cleaned since the last time someone used it. A tiny tin box was sitting in the middle of the chamber. I shuddered, hoping it wasn't someone's cremains, and stifled an *eww*.

"Does George have no family to miss him? That you need to inform?" Dara asked with a bit of exasperation.

"No, no. He's been with my family for generations. He is an orphan, you see, and had worked for us since he was around twelve years old, poor dear. Became an alcoholic, but Father still supported him giving him odd jobs around the house until he worked himself up to caretaker. Our gardens will never be the same now that he's gone. I always thought his alcohol problem would be the end of him. I just had no idea it would be because he decided to take a nip of Father's old potions!" Louise cried. "Now we will have to put him in refrigeration until we are sure Millicent didn't have something to do with his death. What if she gave him Father's elixir?"

How? Like a ghost... no wait. She seemed to be able to manipulate objects and such. Was she like Ellie? Or was she alive and well and doing some significant form of trickery to fool us all?

"Ladies, I am having a hard time believing the pair of you can manage to move bodies and wrangle them down these steps, let alone get them into the retort chamber. How do you manage all this?" I asked, crossing my arms and eyeing them skeptically.

"Oh no! That's what we use Gunther for!" They explained at the same time.

Gunther?

That's when we noticed a large coat rack at the base of the stairs shift and an immense, somber man appear in its place. A shifter!

Ah! We were indeed dealing with the paranormal!

CHAPTER 10

$\mathcal{I}$ woke up late the next morning. I think I got a total of two solid hours of sleep. Earlier, when we finally arrived back at our RVs, the birds were chirping, and the sky was promising a morning where the sun would reign supreme and the clouds would take the backseat.

Ellie never showed back up and while I was concerned, something told me she was gathering evidence or on a little side mission to prove she was an asset to our group. I worry, but it's not as if I can track her down in her ethereal form, nor does she come when called. More's the pity.

As much as we wanted to get back over to the Birch home, we had work to do here. I stumbled around my RV while Bob kept one eye on me as he sunned himself in my sink. The way I was parked allowed a bit of morning light to land just so in the small sink, and Bob felt this the perfect spot for him to catch rays while waiting for me to feed him— or swat at me as I passed to exit the RV. I guessed he wanted that vantage spot if I inadvertently forgot to provide sustenance, making it much easier to score a hit.

Today was his lucky day, however.

I reached into the cabinet and grabbed a can of his favorite food with bits of cheesy goodness in every bite, and also topped off his dry food bowl so he'd have plenty to munch on throughout the day. I felt guilty leaving him alone so often. After a failed experiment of allowing him in my tent as I worked—let's agree to Bob and priceless breakables not mixing—we both decided he would much prefer lounging around in the safety of our home instead.

I cleaned out Bob's water dish and filled it. Then I went over to the driver's cab and removed the visor shade that gave me privacy. At this time of the year, I could still get away with exposing the windshield but come April, things would start to heat up, and it wouldn't be energy efficient, not to mention it would turn my abode into an overheated enclosure.

"Ok, Bob. I'm off. Be a good boy!" I grabbed my thermos of coffee—much needed with the lack of sleep I'd had and went out to greet the day.

"Meorew!" Bob wished me luck. I'd need it.

Heading to the common area where all of us gathered before continuing to our tents, I saw most of my gang were already up and nursing coffees of their own.

"Any news?"

Antoine shook his head no. We'd left Serena and Sydney behind to try and lure Millicent out of hiding and possibly confront Ellie if she chose to appear. Plus, our two minor demons were the perfect choice to exorcise our recalcitrant ghost—or at least get her to show her hand.

"Louise pulled me aside last night after Bella wandered back into the kitchen area," Dara informed us. I remembered she took the two elderly sisters into the parlor to have a chat but didn't have time to follow up with what she found out if anything. With her cleric abilities in full force, Dara had the personality to coax any tale out of even the most hesitant, getting them to share their deepest, darkest secrets with her kind smile and a gentle clasp of her hands to theirs. What most didn't realize, however, was the subtle druid magic she released via her hands which compelled even the most intractable to speak. If that didn't work, she could always zap them with something stronger.

That was our Dara. A sweet, plump, mother figure that could skewer you in a heartbeat then heal you once she got what she wanted out of you!

"She didn't want Esther to overhear particularly, but she wanted me to let our group know how she felt about Millicent. From what she imparted, I'd say Louise felt Millicent had always been a spoiled child and a dangerous one as well. Odd occurrences always seemed to follow the child, and people whispered she practiced dark island magic."

We collectively rolled our eyes at that news such as it was.

"The odd thing is, Esther, pulled me aside a bit later and gave me the same story, only she told me Millicent often tortured small animals then moved on to neighborhood children. Nothing that would do permanent harm, but little things that made one realize she might be a tad unstable. She followed this with a caveat that it was all hearsay as she had never witnessed such deeds."

"Was she ever punished by her parents? Did she say?" Bella asked.

"Well, here's the thing... no adult ever witnessed Millicent being anything other than the perfect darling. She was a stunning child, and Esther informed me her father inferred that the others were jealous and that is why they said such things about her. However, when Esther tried to have her father find the people who'd accused Millicent of such acts, he'd told her to hush and never bring it up again. But he closed with something so ominous, Esther never forgot his words. Mr. Birch told Esther if Millicent was pushed too far, her wrath would destroy them all!"

Sven walked over to the picnic table most of the group was assembled around. "Where is that infernal woman anyway? Is she a ghost? Are the two Birch sisters senile?"

Tor crumbled his Styrofoam cup and tossed it into a nearby trash can. "I don't think Millicent is a ghost. She would have to command incredible strength to manage to appear corporeal to the average human—superpower strength to fool us. I think she is up to something else entirely."

"What do you mean?" I managed to ask without sounded remotely breathless.

What? Can I help it if I was transfixed momentarily by his Adam's apple going up and down while he polished off his coffee then tossed his cup?

"Think about it," he said. "Esther and Louise came home and said they found Millicent dead in her room then before they could call an ambulance, she disappeared. Did you ask them to clarify this while you spent time speaking with them, Dara?"

"Yes, as a matter of fact, I did. Louise found Millicent first and rushed to call Esther. When they both went into her bedroom, they said Millicent was lying still and looked like she had dropped her rosary beads—that's another thing. Millicent identifies as Catholic but with island influence. St. Lucia is her birthplace. When they saw those beads on the floor they knew something was wrong. Upon investigating, they said she was deathly cold but not stiff. Since they spent their lives dealing with the deceased, they knew Millicent had passed."

"But why did they not immediately call an ambulance or the authorities?" Nathara asked.

"They were rattled and descended into the kitchen where

Louise put on water for tea to settle their nerves. Then they rang the servants' bell to call Gunther up and let him know what had transpired. Apparently, Gunther went a bit mad. He was very close to Millicent, and they took time to console him. Gunther insisted they check one more time to make sure she was truly dead, and when they all went back upstairs to check, Millicent was gone."

Nathara was tugging on her lower lip, looking confused. "I don't understand. How did they go from a missing body to Millicent being a ghost? I mean, how does it connect?"

Bella piped up at this point. "Esther insisted Millicent had voodoo magic at her disposal and wondered at that being an explanation. She thinks Millicent did some ritual that would remove her body but keep her there in spirit so she could walk the earth and avenge the love she lost or some nonsense. I have been scouring my notes, but nothing in voodoo practice shows any ability to make a corpse disappear then turn instantly into a ghost."

Tor smiled and nodded at Bella, then continued his theory. "That was what I was getting at. Zombiism isn't what the television shows would have you believe. It is more a state a soul is in before it moves on—a soul who came to a bad end. Souls are vulnerable after a tragic demise and can be taken by powerful sorcerers, known as *boko*. The sorcerer traps the soul in a tiny bottle or, in some variances, a tin can or box or another small container with special meaning and controls their undead body—a body that is no longer alive. Sometimes the soul is bound to a totem, like a frog or a poppet. This is where voodoo doll lore came from. Most of the time, the boko uses the body; other times, however, the sorcerer lets the body rest but uses the soul."

"I assume you are knowledgeable on these practices because you are a sorcerer and have studied different folklore?" Antoine inquired and seemed satisfied with the explanation when Tor nodded yes.

Sorcerers tend to study any and every form of magic known in the paranormal world. They are lifelong students and would equally be at home on the battlefield as in a library. I smiled at the image that popped into my head of Tor, dark glasses perched on his nose, sitting by a fire reading a book. Then I shook my head to clear it of such nonsensical thoughts. I wrinkled my nose and frowned, focusing once again as Tor continued.

"My guess is that Millicent performed some variation of voodoo. Being from St. Lucia, I am unsure what exactly the traditions are, but we may be dealing with something else entirely. I'm thinking she is very much alive but deceiving her stepsisters for one reason or another. That is what we need to figure out. Why is she doing this? To what end?" Tor speculated.

"Obeah. Not voodoo. Millicent must know black magic from her people on St. Lucia then." Dara stated. "It was outlawed but rules the believers and practitioners to this day in the Caribbean. Esther and Louise swore Millicent, as a child, was adept—and dangerous."

Dara paused and gave a slight shudder, then smiled.

"I don't know why this is affecting me. It's not like I believe a little girl could have such power... even in our world, and even with 'the talent,' but Millicent it seems, began training in obeah with the help of her grandmother. Mr. Birch told Esther to mind what she said about and around Millicent lest she bring her wrath down on the household and destroy the family. Now isn't that an odd thing for a man to say about his adopted child?"

"She isn't adopted."

I jumped and turned when I heard Ellie's voice coming

from just over my shoulder. No one else could hear what she said, but I asked her what she meant by that.

"I found Mr. Birch's office. It's hidden behind the retort in a secret room that leads to the outside of the home. There is also an old panel on a spring that pops open, gaining you entry to the basement room with the stairs leading up to the kitchen. I found the old entrance to the basement outside, completely covered in English Ivy. Mr. Birch's office is behind those doors. Millicent is his biological daughter. Her grandmother was a practitioner of obeah. Mr. Birch was fascinated by the island magic and may or may not have done away with his first wife so he could marry his new wife and 'adopt' his bastard child. He was a dark witch."

Well, well, well. Ellie certainly proved her worth—not that I ever doubted her.

CHAPTER 11

"*I* think it's Egyptian."

"Ha! If that is Egyptian, I'm a pharaoh."

I tried not to show my impatience with the couple arguing back and forth in front of me. They had been in my tent now going on twenty minutes. Despite my assurance that the vase they brought was a souvenir from a probable vendor somewhere in Cairo, *and* worthless, the wife insisted they had a priceless treasure. The husband agreed with me and wanted to hurry to the next tent since Antoine could verify if the husband's girlie magazines from the 1950s were the authentic treasure items in their possession.

I didn't even need to remove my gloves and hold the vase to know what I would see—and you couldn't pay me to touch the vintage smut magazines.

I just wanted them gone so we could work on our case.

Freedom came in an unexpected package. Tor cleared his throat upon entering my tent. Bella raised her eyebrows and sat back from the tarot reading she was giving a pair of giggly teen girls. They stopped and stared as well. I told you Tor was something to behold!

"I'm sorry to intrude, but you have an urgent phone call, and you can't put it off," Tor said while giving the couple an apologetic grimace.

"But what about my vase?" the annoying woman lamented.

"Babe. I will buy you another vase just like it at the mall. Come on. I am telling you these magazines can turn quite a profit. Easily enough for that trip to Vegas I promised you."

"Well, we better be staying someplace snazzy on The Strip. I refuse to stay in a hovel." She sniffed.

"We can stay at the Luxor, and you can see some real Egyptian artifacts, babe!"

My head began to ache from all the fake smiling I was doing. *Make them leave. Please make them leave.* I felt like banging my head on the table and gnashing my teeth at the sheer idiocy I just experienced with these two.

When they finally left, lugging two shopping bags filled with images of naked women, I turned to Tor and asked him what, if anything, was wrong.

"You really do have a phone call. Esther only had Antoine's number, but she is insisting she needs to speak with you." I must have handed her the wrong business card from the stack I kept at my disposal, inadvertently giving her Antoine's.

Frowning, I followed Tor over to Antoine's tent and spied my argumentative couple settling at his table. He held out his cell for me, and I thanked him while I went off to the outside of the tents for some privacy and noise reduction. I could already hear the husband going on and on about the 'fine art' in his custody.

Antoine looked exhausted and it was no wonder. While we all got a modicum of sleep, Antoine stayed up and wove the illusion spells needed to keep humans from noticing how unusual some of my team looked. It could be done by the witches in our group, or even Bella, but Antoine insisted, as leader, that he should be the one to do so. Vampires need little if any sleep, getting in large amounts when and if they chose to find a coffin to go snuggle in for a century or two, but I knew he was feeling it right now.

"Esther? It's Maggie. How may I help you?"

"Have you seen today's paper?" she cried, and I was alarmed at the level of stress in her voice. I feared for her health because she sounded like she was about to faint, and I hoped Louise was nearby to help her.

"Uh, no... I don't usually get the paper when I am visiting a town. I usually go on the internet and..."

"You must go look! It's horrible. Just horrible! Millicent is at the bottom of this. I just know it."

"Esther, slow down. Even if I looked at the paper, I don't know what I'd be looking for. Can't you tell me?" I asked. What on earth has the old lady this rattled?

"Oh! I can tell you alright. It's today's obituary. Carolyn Stewart-Hoskins is dead."

I waited to see if she would elaborate and sighed when nothing more was forthcoming.

"Esther, I really am sorry, but why is that important?"

"Carolyn Stewart-Hoskins was Ronnie Stewart's sister."

Again, nothing Esther told me made much of an impact, considering I didn't know who Ronnie Stewart was.

"Ok. And why is this important?"

"Oh! Didn't we tell you his name? Ronnie Stewart was Millicent's beau. The one she was supposed to marry. The one who died in the Korean War."

"Why is this distressing you so? I thought the family moved away and you lost touch. People die, Esther. Every day. What is the real reason you are upset?" I was losing patience by the minute. I like the two sisters, but I found their scatterbrained delusions a bit much to take.

"Carolyn was found hanging in the family backyard... by her brother. Ronnie is alive! Or was. After he called 911 and hysterically reported how he found his sister, the paramedics first on the scene found him lying dead in the backyard, eyes wide open with a look of horror on his face. His obituary is right below Carolyn's! What's more, it seems he choked to death! And Maggie? He had one of my father's old elixirs in his hand! Millicent must have killed them both!"

Oh, well... crud.

* * *

AT THE BIRCH HOUSE, Antoine, Bella, Nathara, and me, along with Dara holding tight to Madame Myna, were assembled around the dining room table.

Despite our hesitancy to show the paranormal to humans, we figured Esther and Louise had grown up around the odd and magical if their father really was a dark witch. They insisted, upon being questioned, that Mr. Birch had dabbled in the arts—the arcane arts—but they had no magical ability whatsoever. That's when Dara gently mentioned Ellie discovering the secret room behind the retort and Mr. Birch's notes on Millicent—and his claim that he was her biological father. When both women blanched, and we feared they'd faint, Antoine had suggested we all take a seat around the table to discuss this further.

Louise was still moaning and fretting over the revelations. Esther started to look angry—like she would spit nails any minute now.

"How could he? All these years and he never thought to inform us before he died? All this time that wretched girl was our half-sister?" I thought this a bit harsh and didn't want to pass judgment on the two sisters. I hoped it wasn't because of intolerance or flat-out racism on their part, how they both reacted to the news. I mean, after all these years, was it so shocking?

Before I left the fairgrounds, I asked Ellie to hang with Bob, who was still feeling left out and sullen. Her company would cheer him up. But before I did, I asked her if she and Millicent had made eye contact on the day we were hustled out of the Birch home when we'd first met the woman. Ellie had indeed believed Millicent could see her because when their eyes made contact, Ellie winked—and Millicent turned white as a sheet making a slight 'oh' sound before recovering.

That didn't sound like a ghost coming face-to-face with a contemporary. It sounded like a living, breathing person confronting a spirit and not knowing what to do about it with the company around—nor how to conceal that she could see such phenomena. I suspect she was surprised but afraid that we might whip out our gear and take over the house again if she reacted. It was better to rush us out and try to deal with the problem in her own way—only Ellie didn't stick around to find out what Millicent would do next.

That was a shame. We might have gotten some insight if Ellie stayed to gauge Millicent's reaction.

Dara had Madame Myna swirling up a storm in her crystal ball. Tiny sparks would trigger lightning as the purple smoke turned darker and darker.

"Heed my warning. Evil is near! The one you trust has betrayed you. The heart clouded by unrequited love can shatter and break. What is left behind is a shell—and dangerous in being scorned."

Esther's frown deepened. "The one we trust. A day doesn't go by where I don't proclaim to Louise just how much I mistrust Millicent. Why she always ran around with a secretive smile and was up to all manner of nasty things!"

Louise looked ashamed of Esther for airing their dirty

laundry. "Esther, dear, Millie wasn't all that bad. She was a sweet child—until she felt slighted. It was only after she went a little mad that we worried she'd gone dark," she chided. "I don't think she was born evil."

"Can you think of anything that would have caused Millicent to act out now? How did she find out about Ronnie... oh! Didn't she say she just became proficient on the computer? She learned how to navigate the internet! What if Millicent recently found out about the deceitfulness of Ronnie's family —not to mention the man himself. After all, his mother and sister lied about his death in the war. But when he returned, why did he not look for Millicent?" Dara wondered.

"Ladies. In recent weeks, how had Millicent been acting? Did anything weird occur that might have caused her to lose her mind as such?" I asked.

Louise tapped her fingers gently on the table then sat back when she recalled something. Snapping her fingers, she gave Esther a knowing look then turned to us.

"That package that arrived before she... well before we thought she'd died. Remember Esther? We asked why she reacted so negatively after opening it. After all, it had some ribbons and a dried flower in it. Oh! And wasn't there a small dried-up lizard as well? I thought it odd for someone to send such a hideously dead thing. It had a tiny bit of yarn tied around its neck. I believe all the items were in some sort of container, like an old cigarette case. Right, sister?"

Esther nodded yes and crossed her arms before angrily spouting her displeasure at having such a thing arrive in the mail. "At least I think it came by post. Millie was sitting on the front porch then came running in with it in her hands. She dropped everything on the kitchen table and accused us of sending it to her. As if we would touch a nasty dead lizard. What nerve to accuse us of such a poor joke! After all, it must have been someone getting back at her. Probably because she was such a naughty brat for years!"

Again, Louise looked nervous and ashamed of Esther's outburst. Of the two, I believed Louise to have a softer spot for their youngest sibling—now that we knew she *was* a sibling!

We spent the hour before this little reading from Madame by going methodically through Mr. Birch's old office and pouring over his notes. He was indeed claiming to be a dark witch, but not a very strong one, and he believed his joining with Millicent's mother might bolster his strength and cause him to grow in power. He did hint that his tonics to help his first wife, Esther and Louise's mother, may have worsened her condition and probably caused her to die earlier than had he left her alone—or moved her to a drier climate.

After the Birch sisters discovered the deceit by their father, Louise became more sympathetic toward Millicent, but Esther became bitter. More so than she had been before. I could understand her ire, but I felt it was misdirected at Millicent and not where it belonged, with her father.

"What happened to the package and its contents?" Antoine queried.

"Oh, I don't rightly know! Now that you ask. Didn't Millie say something about having Gunther 'deal with it" and rush off to find him?" Louise asked her sister.

Esther shrugged and rose from her chair. "Let's ask him."

Gunther lumbered up the basement stairs and followed Esther back into the dining room. When we broached the subject of the items inside the box that Millicent had received, Gunther looked wary and shook his head in the negative. He whispered he'd had no knowledge of what Millicent did with it, nor did she ask him to remove the items from the house.

He looked at Louise then murmured, "Miss Millie got

mad. Miss Millie took the little box and spat on that lizard. You ask Felicia. She knows." Then he begged off back to his basement hideaway but not before bidding us a pleasant day. But before he could make his escape, Esther asked one more question of him.

"Gunther. Did you hear about the deaths in the next county from ours? It seems the Stewart family has come to misfortune. Both Carolyn and Ronnie are dead. Did you know he was still alive?"

Gunther looked shocked than angry before abject sadness crossed his face. "She did him in then. Miss Millie. She had to save face—that she did."

We let Gunther be on his way and pondered what we'd discovered. I also wondered if Gunther transformed into other nondescript objects like the coat rack when not on duty. Shifters could be a weird bunch.

"Who is Felicia?" I asked.

"She is one of our servants, but she hasn't been here in a long while. I will have to ring her and see what she knows," said Esther.

"Could this news be what Madame is trying to warn us about? Do we need to find Millicent and..."

I paused, not wanting to voice what we might have to do to stop the insane woman from continuing her killing spree. Who else could it have been? Although as I thought it, I felt a fissure of uncertainty. After examining my reaction, I assumed I commiserated with Millicent and understood, as such, what it must have felt like to discover the man you thought long dead but had never forgotten was alive and well —and living two towns over from yours. And had been for decades!

Poor Millicent.

This going back and forth on whom I thought might be guilty was making me dizzy!

That wouldn't stop us from bringing her to justice. And if she were the one to wield such power, it would be ours to mete out that justice and not the local police. I shivered as a chill came over me. Something wasn't sitting right with me, and I needed to figure out what was wrong—and quickly.

CHAPTER 12

*A*ntoine decided the household staff—and we found out from the Birch sisters it was only a nurse, a woman who came in twice weekly to clean, the cook, and Gunther—had to clear out lest they fall victim to Millicent if she was on a killing spree. He also had Esther and Louise pack overnight bags and called Sven to come over then take the duo to a nearby hotel where he was to stand guard over them until further notice.

The rest of us were heading over to our camp to strategize our attack plan and have Bella begin concocting wards that would help keep us from harm. She had Serena and Sydney helping her and insisted she'd only need an hour or so, then we could head back to the old Birch Victorian.

Thinking I should probably catch a quick nap in the interim so I'd be ready for a witch fight—or whatever Millicent considered herself, I headed home.

When I arrived at my RV, I fully expected to find Ellie fast asleep with Bob curled up next to her. Instead, I found an irate cat, who'd flipped his kibble bowl onto the floor in protest and no Ellie anywhere. Kicking off my shoes and pulling off my gloves, I placed my hands on my hips and gave Bob an angry scowl.

"You are a naughty cat, Bob! Look at the mess you've made!"

I grabbed my dustpan and tiny broom and swept up the mess, then paused when I noticed the plethora of books open on the table. It looked like Ellie had marked each page with sticky notes, and it seemed the majority of them had to do with obeah magic.

"What have we here?" I sat down and pulled the closest book over to me. I began to read and soon became enraptured with the lore of Millicent's island home. It looked like Ellie discovered Millicent was not entirely of West African and English descent. She was a Carib or Kalinago, native indigenous people on the island before it became St. Lucia. It was called Hewanorra by these tribes. Ellie had opened a small book that I discovered was a diary of sorts from Mr. Birch's library. How had she managed to take the book with her and bring it back here? Ellie was capable of one surprise after another, it seemed.

I continued reading his journal and paused when he mentioned Millicent's maternal grandmother. He had notes on their correspondence throughout the years, and in one instance, the old woman wrote about Millicent's proclivities.

"Vyé ayfé-a mété an modisyon anlè ti manmay-la. The evil fairy put a curse on the child. But she fought hard to stay pure. She is a good girl."

She went on to say Millicent would always be a target because of her talents and warned Mr. Birch not to let his other daughters belittle her granddaughter, for she would put a spell on them.

"Matjé sa mwen di'w-la! Heed what I'm telling you! Millicent is a good girl, but even a good girl can be pushed too far!"

Was Mr. Birch afraid of his own daughter? Oh, Millicent. What happened to you?

I found more notes slipped in the pages of his diary. One letter was from Carolyn and Ronnie's mother and told how she discovered Millicent came from people who believed in 'Satan worship' and black magic. She wanted no part of it and refused to let her son be destroyed by such evil. Another letter was from Ronnie, and it looked like he tried to reach out to Millicent, explaining he had no idea of the pain his family caused her. Still, he believed it too late for them and wouldn't go against his family because he feared they'd make Millicent's life miserable. He signed off that he'd love her forever. I didn't believe Millicent ever saw that note. Especially since Mr. Birch scribbled a short sentence across the front of it: *Why didn't he give this to Millie? Ah! Too late now!*

What a mess. Wait... he? Who was the *"he"* that kept the note from Millicent?

I was beyond tired and knew I'd have to figure this out later.

I stood up to grab that nap before too much more time passed and I lost the opportunity, but that's when my eyes tracked over to the lamp sitting innocently on the opposite side of the table.

"What on earth?" It was the very lamp the Birch sisters brought to me the first day we met—the same one I thought was back on the desk in the library in their Victorian. The same lamp Millicent was purported to be hiding in—which made it all the more stupid that I reached out and grabbed hold of it before realizing too late I'd removed my gloves.

"I'm glad you could join us."

Millicent was sitting on the window seat again. This time

she wasn't keening. This time she had a face. But even as I thought this, I could hear a soft keening circumventing the house and resonating off the very walls. It wasn't loud and jarring like the first time I'd heard her but was more a whispered lament.

Ellie sat on a chair near the desk and looked exhausted. Her dark hair was tousled, and her eyes were set deep as if she'd lacked several nights' rest. I know she didn't really need to sleep, so seeing her so gaunt had me quaking.

"Are you ok?"

"I'm fine, Mags. We have a slight problem."

If I heard that phrase one more time I would start keening myself!

I slid my gaze back toward Millicent, who sat ramrod straight, her derision evident as she bestowed upon me a penetrating stare that would break a lesser person. I was not easily frightened and felt my magic click on. I rarely used my witch side, but I was rather adept at holding my own against another witch when I did. What Millicent was, exactly, had yet to be determined.

"Are you an obeah sorceress?" I asked.

Millicent raised her brows in mild surprise. "You have been doing your homework. My *gwanmanman*, my grandmother, she practiced obeah. I am not as proficient as she."

"But you do practice the dark art?"

"Dark? No. Black magic, dark magic. It's all magic to me. I make no distinction between what one might call light magic versus dark. Magic is magic."

I begged to differ, but ok.

"Are you trying to harm your sisters? Did you kill the Stewarts, Millicent?"

A look of extreme pain crossed Millicent's face, and she slumped a little before straightening her spine once again. "Is that what you think?"

"Honestly? I don't know what to think. I believe an injustice has been done to you, but I am not sure why you would resort to killing two people who thought they were doing something right, at least in their minds. Carolyn to protect her brother after she found out you came from black magic and superstitions, as she put it. Ronnie because he believed it was too late to seek you out after learning of his family's treachery. In the end, he never married, you know."

"I didn't kill them."

We stared at each other for a long minute, but Millicent offered no further explanation.

"What about the trickery you are doing against Esther and Louise?"

"Trickery? I am trying to stay safe from those two! Ever since I first arrived in my new home, they did nothing but terrorize me. No... I take that back. My sisters were never mean, just ambivalent. That uncertainty turned into mistrust and derisiveness, and finally loathing. I never wanted it to be this way. I had sisters! I wanted us to be close! They believed lies about me and became distant and sardonic. It was a lonely life I had in these walls."

"Why then the pretense? What's with the wailing and the faking of your death? You are very much alive, after all."

"Yes. I am. Very much so. I did learn some things from Gwanmanman. I learned how to appear dead, lifeless, and cold. I learned how to slip between the veils and see the Others. Like your sister here."

"You can see ghosts then. I was correct."

Millicent nodded.

"Were you afraid of your father? What of your own mother?"

"My father was a sick man in the head. He wanted power. He hurt my mother. She had me and hoped he'd finally be happy and have what he wanted... a tie to the magic he could never comprehend. But he became more and more insistent that I show him my secrets. Only I did not have any to give him! Father would never have been able to be a boko, to practice obeah. Never. He made my mother ill with his demands. Did Esther or Louise inform you that my mother died in the same manner as his first wife?"

No, they had not revealed this nugget of information. I shook my head.

"So why the intrigue?"

"I'm hiding from them. Somehow, they managed to put a spell on me. They made an Old Higue, a duppie, and brought her here where she wanders, keening and gnashing her teeth. About five years ago, the book my gwanmanman left me went missing. They denied taking it, but they must have, to learn its secrets and then made the duppie. They tied her to me, revealed their deceit, then stole the tin box that holds the magic that binds her to me. If I can't find and destroy those items, the Old Higue will come for me. That's why I am riding the mist between worlds. I'm in hiding. When I was in the mental hospital, something I could have avoided if Esther and Louise hadn't signed my life away, Gunther warned me never to trust my sisters. He believed they were jealous of me. My mother tried hard to be a second mother to the two of them, but their own loss hurt them, I guess. I still can't believe they want to destroy me...but who else would know how to set the duppie after me?"

But... I was almost sure it wasn't the two sisters. But then... who?

"What is an Old Higue...um, a duppie? I've never heard of such a creature."

"She is a wanton evil spirit who will rip the skin from your body and suck the breath of life out of you while you sleep. If the Old Higue gets me, she will turn me to be like her. I will become a duppie. Please, Maggie Fortune. You have to help me!"

"You know I'm not really here, right? That once I let go of the lamp, I will go back and have to drive to your home again."

"I know. But while you are here, can you not look for the package? It was in an old Craven A cigarette tin from the 1950s. They were all the rage in St. Lucia. The minute I opened that tin, and I saw the lizard tied in red yarn... I knew. I *knew*."

"But Millicent. How? How could Esther and Louise learn this? If your father could not, how could they? And why? What motive do they have? They suspect you of deceit. You suspect them. Could there be another person capable of causing this other than your sisters?"

"No. It must be both of my sisters. They never loved me. I'm not wrong, Maggie. They stole my book, my grandmother's book. They must have learned how to cast spells. I'm not wrong. Do you believe me?"

"I don't know what to believe. Why is Ellie here? Did you do something to her?"

"No, Mags," Ellie said. "When I read through that journal and found those notes, I started suspecting someone was doing this to hurt Millicent. Call it ghostly intuition. I reached out with my mind and found her. When she heard me, she touched the lamp, and I came to be here—and I assume the lamp went to you. Only I am not leaving until you get back here for real. Someone has to stay and watch Millicent's back."

"Esther and Louise are with Sven."

"I'm staying, Maggie. Just... please hurry back."

I nodded and went to release the mental hold I had on the lamp, feeling myself hurling back to reality and my RV. Suddenly, I felt a jarring pull and a vibration that shifted my perspective. Instead of winding up back at my place, I found myself sprawled on the grass outside the Birch home, mere feet away from the now revealed entrance to the basement.

That has never happened before! What kind of evil magic was this?

CHAPTER 13

*D*isoriented only for a few minutes, I quickly jumped up and discovered I wasn't delusional or imagining any of this.

Somehow, I was now in the Birch backyard and no longer sitting in my RV. I wondered what poor Bob was thinking after witnessing me disappear before his very eyes. That poor cat. I mentally promised him extra snuggles and treats to make up for what I assume was a rather traumatic event.

Wait. If I was here, that meant Ellie might have gotten whisked back to the RV—or she was right now sitting where I'd left her with Millicent, in the library.

I ran over to the back porch and sighed in relief when the door opened for me.

Heading to the front of the home, I peered into the library and was disappointed and mildly alarmed to find it empty. Where was Millicent? And Ellie? I was about to call out to them when I felt the hair on my arms raise and a shiver course through my body. That's when I turned and saw the faceless woman standing behind me.

Oh geez! I didn't like this no-faced spook. Old Higue did

Millicent say? I briefly wondered if that meant hag, not that I was splitting hairs over the vernacular. The keening began, this time in earnest, although she made no move toward me.

I slowly felt around my person and was astounded. I had managed to snag my cell phone and have it on me throughout this tribulation. Dare I try and reach someone from my team and send for help? I glanced down then back at the gray woman who still hadn't seemed to notice my presence.

Looking down at the screen again, I noticed a few missed messages. They were all from Esther and Louise. *Now* those two had my number, and how the heck do two ninety years olds know how to text?

Get out of the house. We might be wrong about Millie! That was from Louise.

Someone is tormenting this family. I'm not sure Millicent is dead. I think she may be in hiding! I remembered where I saw her tin container and that must mean...

Nothing. No other message came through.

I switched to my favorites list and punched Antoine's number. He immediately picked up and began speaking. "Maggie! Where are you? We've been looking everywhere and..."

"Antoine. No time. Listen, I'm at the *YEOW*!"

I dropped my phone which promptly shattered as the gray Old Higue, or hag or whatever you want to call her rushed me.

One minute she was placid and immobile. The next, she was four inches too close to my face and growling. That's when I noticed a hole open up dead center where an entire face—eyes, nose, mouth, should be. A big, black, gaping maw opened, and she began to suck air in like a Dementor in those Harry Potter movies. I freaked out and spun in the opposite direction, where I ran like a madwoman into the foyer.

I didn't wait to see if she followed and continued through to the kitchen and decided to loop around and head out the front door. Maybe all these doors and openings would buy me time and/or distract her, allowing me to render her harmless.

As I passed the basement door, I came to a sudden halt.

I knew where the tin cigarette box was! Holy cow! It just came to me, and I feared it might be too late to save it if old George had gone up in a puff of smoke and ash. If I was correct, it was the small item I saw sitting in the chamber of the crematory! It had to be.

Giving a quick peek behind me and not seeing the faceless woman, I quietly opened the basement door and crept down the stairs. In the back of my mind, I hoped Antoine understood my plight and whereabouts and had the team coming to my rescue—not that I needed rescuing just yet.

My mind was working overtime. If Louise and Esther thought they were wrong in their accusations toward Millicent, and Millicent was wrong about her two sisters, then who was doing all this?

I made it to the bottom of the steps and walked around to the retort's side panel. It had several buttons and gears. It even had temperature controls and a giant spinning mechanism that counted the bodies that went through the system —just ick.

There was only one button that looked like it might open the machine, so I held my breath and pressed it. Sure enough, the panel opened in front, revealing the chamber where the burning takes place. The box was still there. I was right!

I chided myself the loss of my gloves and cringed inwardly as I had to lean far into the chamber to grasp the tin cigarette box. Imagery began wafting through my mind, but I fought to stay here in the present, although it wasn't easy. I broke out in a cold sweat.

Pulling the item toward me, I stood upright once again and decided to open the box. Inside, it was just as Louise described. A dried flower, hair ribbons in a cerulean blue shade, and a shriveled-up lizard with red yarn around its neck. Poor lizard.

I sent a mental prod to Ellie and told her that I'd found the box. Hoping to avoid detection by the faceless creature, I started up the steps leading to the kitchen when I had a change of heart. Why go that way when I knew I might run into the freaky duppie thingy? I turned and began searching the wall for the secret panel that would lead to Mr. Birch's office and the exit beyond. I had just touched a small crevice on one side of the shelf when a spring sounded, and the door swung open. That's when I came face-to-face with a very disagreeable Gunther.

"Oh! Hello there. I was just heading outside and needed to call Esther and Louise. I have something of theirs here."

The menacing looks the aged shifter was giving me made me realize I might possibly be in a wee bit of trouble. Then everything clicked into place in my mind.

"You are in love with Millicent, aren't you? You kept the letter from Ronnie from ever reaching her. It was you who summoned the duppie and are trying to ensnare her. If Millicent is turned into a duppie, an Old Higue, you can control her by holding these items in this cigarette box, therefore holding Millicent prisoner! Madame Myna was correct, this is about jealously and unrequited love!"

Gunther didn't deny it and I knew I had most of it figured out.

"Give me that box."

Mentally running through the last occasion I took on an evil shifter, I realized I didn't like my odds. Some of them were downright strong, I know Sven was. If not, they could instantly turn into any object or creature they wanted to, and I began to worry. Not enough to render me immobile, but enough to fast-think every step I'd take to pummel the brute senseless and run.

You'd run too, so don't judge!

As I backed away from Gunther, he anticipated my move and lunged. If it weren't for the discarded dumbwaiter base lying in my path, I might have outrun the monster and made it back upstairs. Instead, I went down. *Hard.*

I didn't like the smug look that crossed Gunther's evil visage and did what any woman would do in my situation, paranormal or otherwise. I pretended to cower, and when he lunged for me, I kicked out and landed a direct hit in his happy land.

It would have worked had he not shifted into a jaguar.

Yes. A jaguar.

I felt his teeth sink into my shoulder seconds after rolling to one side, knowing he was aiming for my neck, and I tried not to scream. I released my magic and slammed it into the side of his head. Howling, Gunther shifted into a bat, and he flew upwards and away from me.

I reached up and felt my shoulder. My hand came away covered in blood.

Ok, now I was pissed off.

I jumped up in one quick movement looking every which way for the brute. Where was he? Could he have been so injured by my magic he chose to leave rather than fight me? Really? I still had the tin box and clutched it to my chest as I ran upstairs and into the kitchen. That's when I felt Gunther land on my back and push me to the ground.

The cigarette tin went flying across the floor and stopped just inside the dining room. Pinned to the ground, I didn't like my odds much, so I wrenched my arm in a painful maneuver and reached up to let another round into Gunther's side. Screeching in pain once more, he pulled me up and flipped me over, and that's when I saw what he'd shifted into.

A troll? Really?

Oh, and he was drooling snot globs all over me—like *eww*!

In case you didn't know, trolls were not the oversized monsters you've seen in various movies like Lord of the Rings. They are tall and skinny and leak snot and goo from every orifice. And they smell. Like, honestly smell—like roadkill. However, they *are* powerful, and he pinned me like a weakling on a wrestling mat. He was toying with me at this point because he could have chosen a much deadlier manifestation than a stupid troll! I was pondering all this and wondering why he wasn't attacking me.

That's when he licked my face.

Of course, you know, this means war. Like, flat-out psycho-chick insane-freak-out mode. I didn't even think. I went on the offensive and threw everything I had at his big stupid head. I thrashed and shoved and pulled magic from my core, letting the evil shifter have every bit of my magical wrath. The intensity was too much for Gunther, and I soon had the situation flipped. I was on top of him, giving him the beating of his life. That's how Johnny and Tor found me when they came running in to save the day. I *still* didn't need saving, mind you.

I had the most potent magic in my arsenal coursing through Gunther's head, and he was quickly becoming a vegetable in my clutches. I don't think he realized I was a witch. Perhaps he only heard I was psychic, or maybe he didn't even know that much about me. Either way, it was a mistake on his part for not doing his homework regarding my abilities. I was one minute away from turning the shifter's brain into a pile of ash when Tor looped his arms around my torso and pulled me away from my quarry.

"That's enough, lass. Leave him be. He won't be hurting anyone ever again. Well done!"

Johnny whistled a long low breath out and shook his head at the mess before him. "Goodness, Mags. You're a demon in battle. Why did you never tell us how much power you have in those ungloved hands of yours?"

It was all over before I could get much fun out of it, and I thought we were in the clear, but at that moment, the lady with no face waltzed into the kitchen.

CHAPTER 14

*I*t could have been bad. I wasn't sure if my magic could have touched the creature, especially since I had no idea what an Old Higue was. But on her faceless heels came Ellie then Millicent, with her magical powers on full display, and she managed to subdue the duppie.

At first, I thought she'd been controlling her all along. Which meant she and Gunther were in on this together. Then I understood she knew how to manage the creature with the poppet, the lizard, safely in her possession. Thankfully, she picked up the tin when they rushed in with Antoine right behind them. Millicent and Ellie were stuck on the other side of the veil until I subdued Gunther. He must have used magic to keep them separated from me when I was sucked out of my return and plopped outside the basement door.

None of us knew why wards prevented us from scrying the paranormal upon our initial contact with this household. Wards that prevented us from detecting the magic and power in Millicent and Gunther. It was one of those oddities that might never be answered, although I knew I'd try. It had to have been something Gunther executed. I knew after all the dust settled, I'd need to sit down with Sven and learn more about shifters and the extent of their abilities.

Millicent for her part, admitted she did a minor conceal spell to confound us, but that small amount of magic shouldn't have stopped Sydney and Serena from figuring out what we were up against.

Ah, well, I'd leave that for another day.

After much deliberation, Antoine and I agreed to release the grey woman from the torturous prison she'd lived in these last months. I felt slightly uncomfortable when we dispatched her to oblivion, but Millicent assured me her soul would move on and she would no longer be a duppie.

We'd discovered the woman used to be a household servant, Felicia, turned into a duppie by Gunther, having learned much of the dark magic in Millicent's book.

Gunther's deceit ran deep. It seems not only had he done all that he had, messing with Esther and Louise's medication, and adding a bit of alcohol to their enthusiastic tea consumption— he pitted the three sisters against each other. It explained their confusion regarding Millicent and her purported 'demise.' Millicent had to come to terms that her older sisters weren't the evil twins she ascribed but products of their upbringing. I could tell she was grappling with the overload of information we'd uncovered and wanted to speak with Esther and Louise immediately.

The mood was somber but joyful when there was nothing left to do but reunite the three women and call the police.

Esther and Louise had a tearful and apologetic reunion with their little sister. While it would take time for all the wounds to heal, I truly believed the tale of the two sisters would now become one about three, hoping they'd have what little was left of their lives to grow closer. I knew it would be more difficult for Esther than it would Louise, but

I believed the trio would attempt to shake off the old adage that you couldn't teach an old dog—or in this case, old sisters —new tricks.

Prejudices from the past could be dealt with and new bonds forged. They were family, after all. In light of that fact, most of the family's strife resulted from their father having an unnaturally toxic desire for power that was more than enough to bring the sisters closer together even at their lofty ages. They couldn't erase all the hurt their father caused, nor could they get their mothers back—but they could move forward and not let their father's evil taint what time they had left.

Antoine had to do what he did best. Connect the dots for the local police, allowing them to close the case on the Stewart family double murder. We used a draining spell to extract the magic from Gunther, sapping him dry so he would no longer be able to shift. Dara healed him just enough that he could stand trial as a human and be sent to prison. His fingerprints were all over both victims, so the police didn't have many dots to connect, especially once the Birch sisters made up a long and sordid tale of jealousy and woe.

I'm still not one hundred percent certain Officers Wilkins and Anand believed everything they were told, but the higher-ups seemed satisfied with our explanation. Millicent's word obviously had much hubris behind it. That and the donations from the sisters over the years and their family name, made some of the lingering questions dissolve. The satisfaction of having a horrible murder case be closed in a hurry was agreed on by all.

None of us was concerned Gunther would start talking about us or his past, or his part in this tale. Who would believe him? He lived a life of deceit, pining for a woman who would never return his love—or what he believed to be love anyway. He admitted to killing poor George, my friendly stiff in the window seat, and the Birch sisters' life-long caretaker and handyman. He didn't give his reason for giving the teetotaler a bottle of Mr. Birch's elixir that not only contained alcohol but enough poison to drop a troll—pun most definitely intended.

Once this came to light, and all our questions were answered, as much as any question as to why someone would do the things they did could be answered, Ellie used an enormous amount of magic at her disposal to pull selective memories from Gunther. She made him not only forget about us but suggest he keep what he knew and did to himself and not reveal our world. It would have to do, I suppose.

Gunther would never be a free man ever again. Nor would he even regain his shifter ability.

The house would go up for sale since all three women decided to retire to an upscale assisted living facility. Who am I kidding? It was more like a dream resort that catered to all your needs. I guessed when you had the money, you could buy such luxuries even at the end of your life's journey. I hoped the three Birch sisters had many years ahead of them. They needed time to heal. While I was still soured at the jealousy Esther and even Louise held regarding Millicent, I knew she wouldn't hold it over their heads. All she ever wanted was a family and her Ronnie.

Millicent transformed before my eyes when I turned the letter from Ronnie over to her and she read his words. If only we could have stopped Gunther sooner, she might have reunited with her lost love. Even for a few years.

I hoped someday their souls might cross paths once more and they'd get another chance at love.

Millicent informed us that Esther and Louise wanted to travel a bit and introduce her to some of their mortuary

111

acquaintances. I was surprised to hear them speak of heading down to Sweet Briar, Georgia, where our cousin Lily Sweet and the rest of the family lived. Something about paying a visit to a Hester and Chester Soule—and their funeral home or some such. I'd have to have them stop by and say hello to Lily for us.

Speaking of mortuary services, we all felt duty bound to pay our last respects to George since he had no one else to do it. We made quite the group as they interred his cremains to the Birch family plot in town, followed by quite the spread at a local restaurant.

Now we were finished with the tale of two sisters who'd stopped in with a unique mystery. I was ready to move on.

My shoulder ached a bit even though Dara did her best druidic cleric-healing magic on me. But I knew that the pain would eventually subside, and I'd be back to my old self again shortly. No one had an answer for me on how I came to be outside the Birch home. What manner of magic caused me to be strewn from one reality to another and have me travel through space like that? It looked like more research was needed and it gave me another question to ask my Aunt Morwena when I reunited with her soon.

Ellie was basking in the glory of a job well done. My entire team of stellar monster-hunters was handing out praise like it was candy, and Ellie ate it up. We were having a cookout while the crew broke down the tents and began packing the gear readying our troupe for the next locale. The main antique and appraisal business had moved on to Knoxville, but we'd spent the extra few days here tying up loose ends and sending old George off with a bang—or puff of smoke as it were.

That thought didn't stop the smell of hamburgers and bratwurst that filled the air near our section of the fairground from making me drool, and I, for one, was looking forward to relaxing in the next few days. Especially since we didn't have far to go.

"One more stop, and this time next week we will be in North Carolina, then we head home. Are you ready to see the family again?" Ellie asked me while she looked longingly at the hamburger I was consuming.

"I think I am. I want to pick Aunt Morwena's brain and see if she knows anything about what happened to me as well as more about the obeah magic and the island culture. It is fascinating and worth having in our knowledge base. Millicent comes from strong stock and their magic is worthy of mention, if not given outright respect. I for one, want to learn as much about it as I can."

Ellie agreed then stretched, causing her arms to waver then turn to mist before solidifying again.

"Are we good?" I asked her.

"Of course, we are! Why do you ask?"

"I don't know, sis. For a while there, I felt like you might be doubting your worth in our little band of nutcases. You're cracked like the rest of us. Never doubt it. And don't forget it."

Ellie smiled and I could see unshed tears threatening to cascade down her spectral face. Instead, she blinked them away and stood up, brushing off imaginary dust from a body that couldn't be affected by such. She grabbed me in a quick hug that never failed to astound me. Hugging a ghost was a unique experience and I couldn't begin to describe it—other than it felt like a million icy-cold butterfly wings descending on you in a cascade of misty wonder.

Giving me a knowing glance, she drifted off just as Tor approached me, looking upbeat that we were heading out soon but wary at the same time.

"What's up?" I was surprised at my ease and non-foot-in-the-mouth ability, wondering where awkward Maggie ran off to.

"I just wanted to tell you how impressed I was with how you handled Gunther. I've never seen such skill and I kind of wished you could have kept tossing him around the place for a bit longer. It was, um..." Tor stopped what he was saying, but just then, Johnny leaned over from his position just behind me.

"What he's trying to say is you were totally hot. A real badass taking down that asshat. And he's turned on a bit. Hell... we all are!"

"Speak for yourself." Ah! Nathara wouldn't let a comment like that go without challenge.

It felt good to be surrounded by my people. Our select group, a hodgepodge of paranormals bent on seeking justice and ridding the world of one more monster in the ongoing battle of good versus evil. There weren't too many places I'd rather be right now.

Even with Nathara in the mix.

Just as I was about to tease Tor playfully, something I didn't think I could have pulled off had I not gained confidence in my baddie-kicking abilities, I happened to glance at the steps leading into my RV. Something shiny caught my eye and I arose, leaving a puzzled Tor in my wake. As I approached the stairs, I once again had the prickly sensation cover my body, making my hair stand on end.

This couldn't be. My mind fought with what it was seeing —even as I crept closer and closer. I wanted to run to Ellie and hold her like I did when we were little, and a thunderstorm had my usually fearless sibling turn from a warrior to a trembling mess, incapable of controlling her fear of the virulent weather.

What could this mean? Was he here? Did he find us again? I had a million questions and no way to know the answers. I just knew things were about to get dicey in our world yet again.

For there, on the step that I was sure was free of anything just moments earlier, was a teeny tiny figurine of a crouching wolf.

THANK YOU FOR READING! I hope you loved meeting Maggie, Ellie, and the rest of the characters. The next book in the Fortune-Telling Twins series is Double Toil and Trouble. Knoxville is the next stop for the antique caravan, and it seems the welcome committee includes rival witch covens and opposition to the odd and outré side of the antique business. If that isn't enough to keep Maggie busy, it seems Nathara is acting suspicious and might be involved in murder!

CLICK HERE TO READ DOUBLE TOIL AND TROUBLE NOW>

And if you enjoyed A Tale of Two Sisters, you'll love reading about Maggie and Ellie's cousin, Lily Sweet, a naïve dark witch who discovers her powers, and reunites with the family she never knew, while coming to terms with her topsy-turvy magical ability. Home Sweet Witch is Book 1 of The Lily Sweet Mysteries and is FREE on Kindle Unlimited!

"Excellent."

- Butterfly & Birch Reviews.

I'D APPRECIATE your help in spreading the word, including telling friends and family. Reviews help readers find books!

Please leave a review on your favorite book sites, like Amazon and Goodreads. THANK YOU!

You can also join my Facebook Group: Author Bettina M. Johnson's Team Wicked for exclusive giveaways and sneak peek of future books—and just plain silliness!

SIGN UP FOR BETTINA M. JOHNSON'S NEWSLETTER: http://eepurl.com/gZKo51

Continue on for a short excerpt from Double Toil and Trouble...

Double Toil and Trouble

Prologue

Do you have it? Give it. Now! Don't tell anyone—or else!

Why did she get involved with this chaos in the first place? She knew better. The betrayal that was coming would change her world forever. Destroy the group of people who had been like family ever since she'd joined them, ever since they welcomed her into the fold. But it wasn't like she had a choice. Not really.

The exchange was made on a rainy night in a back alley behind a small neighborhood dive bar. Not the usual establishment she would ever dream of associating with. Nor the type of people who she found herself indebted to. They went far beyond rough around the edges. These were cold-blooded killers and there were no second chances. No turning back. No do-overs.

Now, wandering haphazardly across recently unearthed cobblestones as she crossed the street, two intricate glass bottles her precious cargo, she felt nothing. She could no longer allow herself to feel. She was in a strange city but could tell this was a transition area, some sections more dangerous than others. Just a few blocks away would find her on the historic Gay Street in the heart of Knoxville, but this was not a good neighborhood. She could feel eyes tracking her progress.

A few panhandlers were working the corner as she approached, and she decided to continue past and not cross the street in a display of weakness. The I-40 overpass was just ahead as she continued up Broadway where she'd left her vehicle. She wondered briefly if it would still be there or what condition it would be in. She'd left it near the Salvation Army building in hopes that would leave it untouched. That she'd stolen it from the parking lot near the bus station didn't matter, she just hoped to return it in one piece to the hapless unsuspecting owner.

"Got a dime, lady? Got a dime? You have some money? I'm hungry."

"No, sorry. I have nothing."

"Got them bottles in your hand. Is that something to drink? You keepin' it all to yourself?"

Refusing to speak to the aggressive man who reached his hand out and began begging for something she couldn't provide, she realized too late she might have to use her magic to stay safe. Something she was trying to avoid. Sighing inwardly, the woman knew she might just blow it all with this little mistake as the unkempt man got in her face and pulled a knife.

"You don't want to mess with me."

The man smiled, showing a mouth devoid of teeth. The reek of filth and alcohol poured off of him and offended her nostrils. She had no quarrel with this poor soul, but he instigated the necessity to use force.

"Oh, I think I do. Gimme that stuff."

She watched as two more homeless men stood up and shuffled in their direction. This was definitely not good. She had to stop this now before things got out of her control. Holding her precious cargo tightly in one hand, she raised the other and sent a spark of magic cavorting around the sidewalk.

The woman observed with little emotion as it slammed into each man, rendering them harmless—not killing them, just making them immobile. It would have been enough, but just then a counterattack came from the side of the building and magic narrowly missed her as she sidestepped the surprise attack.

Magic? Could one of the others have followed her back? Or did she happen to be that unfortunate to find a group of homeless that concealed a paranormal being? She had no choice now and let loose a barrage of magic then turned and ran as fast as she could in the direction of her car. No counterattack followed, and she was not surprised. What she let loose wasn't intended to leave survivors or witnesses.

The smell of charred flesh receded the further away she ran. Reaching the vehicle, she threw open the door, jumped in, then tore off up the street and took a left, almost causing the tires to go up onto the curb.

It was a short drive to the bus station and as she neared the building she began to relax.

That was unfortunate back there, but what could I do? I have to win. Everything I believe in, everything that matters, is tied to this deal.

Slowing down as her destination grew near, the woman

breathed a sigh of relief. She made it. She was safe. Now all she had to do was sit back and watch the end of the world she'd grown so very fond of. A small price to pay for what was to come.

She doubled the trouble and it paid off. All her hard work would pay off.

Eventually.

SOCIAL MEDIA LINKS

I write in my own style that may not be everyone's cup of tea —so if you enjoy my characters and humor, my plots, how the storyline is developing, etc. and are eagerly anticipating the next in the series, be aware that I am just as excited as you are—I've found someone who thinks my story ideas are neat! That is thrilling for any writer to know (or it should be). THANK YOU!

Visit my official website to receive updates, find out about special offers and new releases, or read my blog about writing and farm life - complete with photos - you might even catch me mowing my ten acres (seriously): http://www.bettinamjohnson.net

For more information or to contact me:
author@bettinamjohnson.net

For even more (if you just can't enough of me) follow my
Social Media Links

Mailing List - https://bit.ly/2BvQXmP
BookBub - https://bit.ly/2Epejwj
Goodreads - https://bit.ly/3aTejQW
Author Page - Amazon - https://amzn.to/3lj7L2L
Instagram - https://bit.ly/2QpZa01
TikTok - https://bit.ly/2PQa6Hg
MeWe - https://bit.ly/36A2RcM
Facebook - https://bit.ly/3gOaFZY
Twitter: https://bit.ly/3jahMgY
YouTube - https://bit.ly/2Stvy2X

ABOUT THE AUTHOR

I always knew I wanted to write. As a kid, way before the technology age had hit, I'd be stuck in the car with the folks as we drove from our home on Staten Island, NY, where I was born and raised, to our family property in the Catskill Mountains. To drive away boredom, I would sit, staring out the window, and create adventures of daring thieves riding horseback along the road, trying to escape the law. Other times I'd imagine a wild girl riding her unicorn into battle (I had a vivid imagination - we didn't have video games yet!).

As the years passed, I'd start writing a book, then stop, then start again only to let life get in the way, until one day I had an epiphany—a kick in the pants moment. If I waited any longer, all those wonderful characters in my head would never have their stories told, and that made me sad. So, I treated writing as my career. Once I started, it became apparent nothing would ever stop me again. YOU, dear reader, are stuck with me until I go off to that great library in the sky...or wherever writers go when they crumble to dust in front of their typewriters (or laptops...whatever!).

I live in the North Georgia mountains on what I like to call a farm, with my husband and almost adult kids, a Cairn Terrier, a bunch of cats, and fish. Occasionally other critters show up to keep things exciting.

BOOKS BY BETTINA M. JOHNSON

The Lily Sweet Mysteries:

Home Sweet Witch

Witch Way is Up?

How To Train Your Witch

Sweet Home Liliana

Witch Way Did He Go?

Revenge is Sweet, Witch

Witch and Peace (Coming Soon)

The Fortune-Telling Twins Mysteries:

A Tale of Two Sisters

Double Toil and Trouble

Fire and Earth, Sisters at Birth (Coming Soon)